PONY EXPRESS

When fifteen-year-old Jack Taylor is offered a job with the newly formed Pony Express Company, it looks as though he will be able to rescue his family from the financial problems that are troubling them. However, he injures his ankle, and it is likely his job will fall through. His twin sister, Beth, decides to go in his place . . . and this is the story of the only girl to ever ride for the Pony Express.

Books by Harriet Cade
in the Linford Western Library:

THE HOMESTEADER'S DAUGHTER
THE MARSHAL'S DAUGHTER
TEACHER WITH A TIN STAR
SADDLER'S RUN

HARRIET CADE

PONY
EXPRESS

Complete and Unabridged

LINFORD
Leicester

First published in Great Britain in 2016 by
Robert Hale
an imprint of The Crowood Press
Wiltshire

First Linford Edition
published 2019
by arrangement with
The Crowood Press
Wiltshire

A catalogue record for this book is available
from the British Library.

ISBN 978–1–4448–4073–5

Published by
F. A. Thorpe (Publishing)
Anstey, Leicestershire

Set by Words & Graphics Ltd.
Anstey, Leicestershire
Printed and bound in Great Britain by
T. J. International Ltd., Padstow, Cornwall

This book is printed on acid-free paper

1

My family, which is to say my mother and me and my brother, lived in the town of St Joseph in 1860. This was at the end of the railroad line in those days and so was an important point for those heading off to California or the new territories. Me and my brother were twins and we looked as alike as two peas in a pod. Whether I was a boyish sort of girl or he was a girlish sort of boy, I don't rightly know, but the fact is if we hadn't worn different clothes and one of us with long hair and the other short, you would have been hard pressed to tell us apart. We were fifteen, coming up to sixteen in that year.

My pa had been killed when we were twelve. I don't recollect that we were ever given the details of this unfortunate event, but I do recall that he was shot in a bar-room somewhere in town. I never heard why. One thing I *do* know is that we were left with a whole heap of debts after his death. Neither he nor my mother had any idea of how to handle money and those three years, between his death and the time of which I am about to tell you, were hard. We all three of us had to work and make money as best we could.

One day my brother came home and said, 'Look here! This is the very thing for me.' He took out from his jacket a crumpled little poster which he had pulled down from a post where it had been pinned. There was a picture of a boy on horseback and under it some printed words. We smoothed it out and read the following:

Pony Express
St Joseph, Missouri to California
in *10 days or less*
WANTED
YOUNG, SKINNY, WIRY FELLOWS
not over eighteen.

Must be expert riders, willing
to risk death daily. Orphans preferred.
Wages $50 per month
Apply, PONY EXPRESS STABLES
St Joseph, Missouri

Ma said to my brother, 'Well, you ain't no orphan, Jack, so I reckon that lets you out. Besides, mark what it says here about risking death daily. I do not care for the sound of this business at all.'

Jack said, 'First off is where I am half an orphan, on account of my father is dead. But that don't signify overmuch in any case, Ma. It does not say that you *have* to be such, only that it is preferred. Look though at what they are offering.'

My mother read out the figure of fifty dollars in amazement.

'Why' she exclaimed, 'You are only making a dollar a week at that building you are working on. It would take you nigh on a year to collect fifty dollars. Are you sure it is not a mistake?'

Notwithstanding my mother's apprehensions about that part of the notice touching upon death and orphans, it was agreed that my brother Jack would apply for a job with the new company. Our creditors were pressing and if we did not find some more money soon, it was beginning to look as though our only option would be to dig up and leave town without furnishing anybody with a forwarding address.

I guess I should say a few words about how we were living that March in the year of 1860. We had a little place on the edge of town, with some land around it. This property was heavily mortgaged, which was the chief of our debts. My father had raised money on it shortly before his death and we had no means of paying back the principal. It was all we could do to keep up with the interest payments. Me and Jack had ponies and had both ridden almost as soon as we could walk. The shoeing and suchlike were paid for by lending the horses out to a livery stable from time to time.

'I guess it will be all right,' said my mother, as we talked over the Pony Express idea while Jack was at work. 'Surely, they would not advertize a job of that sort if it were not perfectly safe. Perhaps the mention of risking death was meant by way of a joke.'

'It will be fine, Ma,' I told her. 'Jack can ride like the wind and if it comes to danger of death, he is a dab hand with a pistol as well as being a good rider.'

This seemed to set my mother's mind at rest and we carried on working. It is nothing to the purpose to relate what we were doing to make money at that time, but I will mention it anyway. My mother was taking in sewing from people in town, Jack was hiring out by the day to do rough work such as digging and I was making little boxes, jars, vases and also trinkets to wear. How this came about is a curious story in itself.

Near to our place was an Indian family, who were living in a little log cabin, the kind of thing you might expect Abe Lincoln to have grew up in. They were Cherokees, but I don't know how they fetched up in St Joseph, so far from their homeland. Anyways, there was a little girl who was roughly the same age as me. Although her English wasn't nothing remarkable and I didn't know a word of Cherokee, still and all we became friends. Her father worked in town but she and her mother made little baskets, boxes, vases and trays out of pretty well whatever come to hand and these they would sell in the market. Mostly, they would use birch bark, willow switches, twigs and suchlike and those items they made looked as neat as anything you might buy in a shop. They would decorate them with feathers, dried grasses and so on.

After a while I learned to make stuff that way as well, although it was nothing compared with what she and her mother turned out. But then they were Indians and I guess they had been

6

learning that kind of thing for hundreds of years. Howsoever, I got pretty good at it and used to sell the things I made to people changing stage on their way east or west.

None of the three of us were getting much from all these various enterprises. If we had five dollars a week coming in, that was not a bad week for us. Otherwise, it was a dime here and a nickel there. I relate this in order that you will understand the amazing news that my brother could end up earning fifty dollars a month for just riding. It looked like it could rescue us from all our worries, at least on the financial side.

To cut a long story short, my brother was interviewed by William Russell himself. Russell knew what a set of rascals boys that age can be and he made sure that he would weed out any obvious rogues. He enquired closely into their background and raising, so that he could identify those who would be prone to fighting, stealing and suchlike. Another thing he was particular about was that none of the boys could weigh in at more than 135 pounds. This was to keep up the speed of the ponies. Each boy that was taken on had to swear an oath to Russell. My brother told me that he had to stand there with his hand on the Bible and say:

'I, Jack Taylor, do hereby swear, before the Great and Living God, that during my engagement, and while I am an employee of Russell, Majors and Waddell, I will, under no circumstances, use profane language, that I will drink no intoxicating liquors, that I will not quarrel or fight with any other employee of the firm, and that in every respect I will conduct myself honestly, be faithful to my duties, and so direct all my acts as to win the confidence of my employers, so help me God.'

William Russell was a religious man

and he also gave each boy a Bible of his own. There was a practical reason behind all this and that was, that if any of those young men took to drink or began brawling, it could interfere with the smooth running of the whole system. He thought that if they were reading scripture on a regular basis, they might be less apt to get into mischief.

After taking the oath and being engaged, my brother came home and told us, 'Well, I reckon that has solved our money troubles for a spell. I will be riding out for eighty miles at a trip, changing horses every ten miles. It is money for nothing.'

My mother was still not convinced, saying to him, 'I hope that Mr Russell will not really let you be in danger of death. This does not sound like a respectable business. I hope the neighbours will not talk.'

'I don't see why it should only be boys in on this game,' I said, 'I can ride as well as you any day of the week and better sometimes. I would like to sign up too.'

My brother laughed at that, saying, 'Ha, imagine a girl riding so! It is not to be thought of. She would be stopping every few yards to check her appearance and so on.'

We exchanged a few sharp words after he said this and then I threw myself upon him and we fell to the ground wrestling, until Ma said, 'You two don't cease that, I'll take a riding crop to the pair of you. You ain't so old that I can't whip you.'

Now to understand the next part of the tale, you need to bear in your mind that old saying: the one as touches upon counting chickens before they even hatched out of their eggs. The three of us were living on such slender means at that time that the prospect of having fifty dollars a month suddenly coming to us was quite intoxicating. We owed a heap of money, and not just to the bank that owned the mortgage on our house. We were forever soliciting credit from the butcher, the baker, the candlestick-maker and anybody else who would advance us goods without first having had sight of any cash money. In short, that first month's fifty dollars had been spent before my brother even set off for his first ride. That's how it is sometimes, when folk are as hard up as we were in those days.

So there it was, the whole family was now depending upon my brother Jack to restore our fortunes. You can picture, then, our dismay when he took a tumble while fooling around play-fighting with some friend of his and sprained his ankle so badly that he couldn't put his weight on that leg. Like I said earlier, we'd all been counting on that first month's wages and making plans for spending the money he'd earn after that first month. The consequence was that we all felt keenly that we had actually lost something by his mishap and that our family had been deprived of something to which it was entitled: namely that fifty dollars a month that we believed would have been coming in our direction.

'Lordy,' said my mother, the evening after this accident. 'Just when I began to believe that things might be going in our direction for a novelty and now this happens. We surely must be the unluckiest family hereabouts.'

'Don't take on so, Ma,' I told her. 'It'll come out right in the end, you'll see.'

'I'm blessed if I know how,' she replied. 'We never been deeper in debt. Why, that first month's money would have pulled us clear and set us on an even keel again. After that, we'd have been in clover, with fifty dollars amonth coming in regular.'

My brother Jack didn't say anything. He felt guilty about having fooled around and hurt himself so he missed the opportunity. There was no point waiting 'til his leg was healed and then him going after the job again. There were any number of others who were after those jobs and it was only because he'd been so quick off the mark in applying that he'd got the position in the first instance.

It was then that the first stirrings of an idea came to me. At first I thrust the notion back out of my head, because it was so crazy that it wasn't really worth entertaining the scheme for a second. But then it came back again and I thought to myself, why wouldn't it work? It has to be worth a try, because we wouldn't lose anything, even if it didn't come off.

I said to Jack, 'Nobody at the Pony Express office knows aught yet about you doing your ankle so, is that how the matter stands?'

'I thought at first that it might heal up in time, which is to say by April the fifth. But I don't look for that to happen now, not by looking at the state of my shin and ankle.'

'So you've told nobody?' I pressed him patiently. 'Nobody at the office knows that you aren't going to be turning up there to ride out next Thursday?'

At this point, my mother intervened, saying, 'Happen you best let them know about it son, so's they can make other arrangements. I don't like to think o' letting folk down.'

This didn't at all accord with my own plans and so I said, 'No Ma, I don't think we should do that.' My mother looked at me enquiringly and I said haltingly, reasoning the case out as I spoke, 'What's to hinder *me* riding out on that pony on Thursday? I'm as good a rider as Jack, any day o' the week and I can shoot straighter than him as well. I could keep his job going until his ankle's better.'

There was a dead silence when I'd finished speaking, broken only by Ma saying, 'Of all the crazed schemes I ever did hear of in my life, that has to be the winner. What ails you, child, that you should even talk so?'

I had expected Jack to be dead set against the plan, on account of we were

14

always fighting and each of us mocking anything the other put forward, but he sat up straighter and said, 'Beth, that is one solid gold idea. I reckon as my ankle will be well enough for riding in two weeks, always provided that I rest up and don't put any weight on it for that time. Thursday's five days away, so all you'd need do is ride for nine days and then I could take over.'

'I thought better of your sense, Jack,' said my mother sharply, 'Don't encourage her in this lunacy.'

'But it ain't lunacy at all, Ma,' said my brother. 'Don't you see, it's the best thing in the world. Beth's right, she can ride as well as me and shoot better, too.'

I was pleased to hear him confess this. In the normal course of affairs my brother would sooner have been torn apart by wild horses than admit that a girl could shoot better than him. But this was by way of being an emergency and was no time for polite pretence. If we were to pull this off, then it would

15

need plain speaking and common sense.

'I never heard the like,' said Ma. 'Has the child bewitched you or what?'

Slowly though, we talked my mother round and showed her that this was the only way of rescuing ourselves from the situation. We were in desperate need of that fifty dollars a month that we'd been counting on and without it, it was hard to see how we'd be able to manage. The very real prospect was staring us in the face: of having the bank foreclose on the mortgage and turning us out of our house.

It was this grim possibility which I think finally decided Ma in favour of what I was suggesting. Not that she was keen on it, mind, but it was about the only way out of the hole we were in. The idea of this fifty dollars a month had come just as we were out of options and now to see it being snatched from us in this way was cruel.

'You say that these pony folk were only wanting you to travel eighty miles from here?' asked my mother of Jack. 'If Beth goes ahead with this wild idea, she ain't going to be expected to ride all the way to San Francisco or anything like that?'

'No Ma,' said Jack, trying to hide his smile, 'that would be a good long way. No, she'd ride eighty miles west, changing mounts every ten, fifteen miles or so and then ride back again in the same way. It's money for nothing.'

I was at that time a little hazy myself on the distances and routes of this business. I don't believe that I had ever been more than twenty miles from St Joseph in the whole course of my life and although I'd heard of cities like San Francisco and so on, they meant no more to me than if they'd been in China. But years later I learned about the background to all this and so maybe if I explain some of it, it will make it easier to understand what later befell me.

Until that Pony Express started up it took twenty-four days to get a message from New York or Washington to California. When I was born it had taken more like two months. It was the Butterfield Overland Mail, which began running in the fall of 1858, that shaved the time below a month for the first time. Of course, there were railroads and telegraph wires running here and there, but nothing of that sort west of St Joseph. Just 2,000 miles of empty land, full of deserts, mountains, Indians and I don't know what-all else. So the idea of having a faster way of sending messages to California was greeted with enthusiasm.

The man who really got things moving was a fellow called William Gwin, who was the first senator for California. He was worried that his state was getting left behind the rest of the union, and only hearing of what had been going on in the rest of the country a month or two after everybody else. Gwin had an old friend called William Russell, who happened to be a partner in a firm of wagoners called Russell,

Majors and Waddell. After William Gwin spoke to his friend and put a little money into the enterprise, Russell persuaded his partners to start cutting into the Butterfield's business and so they came up with the notion of the Pony Express.

Like I say, I knew nothing of all this back in March 1860. All I had in mind was to help out my family by hanging on to that fifty dollars a month that we so desperately needed to stave off our creditors and keep the wolf from the door. I asked Jack what I would be expected to know if, that is, I was going to pull this off and pretend to be him. He thought about it for a spell, scratched his head, and then said,

'I don't mind that there's much *to* know. There's a kind of leather thing called a *mochila* and that gets thrown over the saddle. When you change horses, it's just slung on to the next pony you're using.'

'What does it look like?' I asked.

'It's a mailbag, I guess. With four

pouches at each corner. All of 'em are kept shut with little padlocks.'

'What about this changing horses? Won't I have to talk to folk and such? They might guess I'm not you, d'you think?'

'No,' said Jack, 'I don't look for that to happen. From what I can make out, you'll just jump off the one pony and then, when the *mochila's* laid over the saddle, you mount up and are off again. You won't hardly have a chance to speak.'

'And you say I'll need to change mounts every ten, fifteen miles?'

'Sure. Then, when you're eighty miles from here, you just turn back and carry another bunch of mail heading back east. There's nothing to it, sis. All you have to do is be able to ride like the wind and you can do that well enough'

It was funny having Jack reassure me in this way. After all, the whole scheme had been my idea in the first place! Maybe though, I hadn't really thought that anybody would take it seriously.

That first boy who set out west from St Joseph was a big event in the town. His name was Johnny Fry and he was by way of being a friend of my brother's. There was a band playing near the stables and William Russell and one of his partners, a man called Alexander Majors both gave speeches, as did the Mayor of St Joseph. This went on for some time and it looked to me as if everybody in the whole town had turned out to watch. I kept right at the back, because I didn't want to draw attention to myself. I was able to see this *mochila* that Jack had told me of and, as he said, it just lay snugly over the saddle. William Russell shook hands with Johnny and then the mayor shook hands with him and then Alexander Majors shook hands with the mayor and the mayor shook hands with William Russell and after that a cannon was fired and Johnny Fry was off like an arrow out of a bow.

The first leg of the journey was a mere half-mile, to the ferry across the

Missouri into the Kansas Territory. The boat, which I recollect was called the *Denver*, already had a full head of steam, and the second Johnny was aboard it crossed the river.

The one thing which made me uneasy was what would happen if there was all this fuss and commotion in two days' time, when I was going to pass myself off as my brother Jack? I didn't rightly fancy trying to fool somebody who'd actually set eyes on him before. I later found that he'd only spoken to William Russell himself and that Russell had more important things to do than supervise every departure of a Pony Express rider after that first one. Fact is that, when I showed up at the stables forty-eight hours later, there were no bands, mayors shaking hands, large crowds or cannons being fired. Nobody gave me a second glance.

2

Ma was still not happy about my plans and did not scruple to tell me so. The day after the first Pony Express rider left town, she said,

'You'll do what you will do, Elizabeth, as was always the case. You was the same when you were a little girl. I could sometimes slap your brother and make him do my bidding, but it never worked on you. But I ain't easy in my mind 'bout this idea and that's the God's honest truth.'

'It'll be fine, Ma,' I told her. 'You'll see. It's only for a week, 'til Jack's leg has healed. I won't be above eighty miles from here. The next station in the line is Seneca.'

'Promise me to take care of yourself, child. Don't take any chances and be sure to come back safe and sound.'

I went over to my mother and gave

her a hug, which wasn't the sort of action I was prone to as a rule. Then I followed it up by kissing the top of her head. She looked surprised, but pleased, at this unusual display of affection on my part and said, 'You can be the sweetest girl sometimes, Beth.'

Jack's first ride was supposed to depart from the Pony Express stables on 5 April, and so the night before I got my mother to help cut my hair short. She grumbled about it, but then brightened up somewhat when I told her we could sell the hair to a fellow in town who made wigs and suchlike for wealthy ladies. Between the two of us, Ma and I managed to get my hair looking pretty much like Jack's.

The clothes I was to wear were no problem, me and Jack was the same height and I wasn't overly developed up above. When I had his pants and shirt on and with my hair cut short, both he and Ma said that it was positively uncanny how much I resembled him.

'You better not talk much,' said Jack.

'Just kind o' grunt when folk speak to you. 'Sides which, I don't think there'll be time for talkin'. It'll be just jumping from one mount to another at the relay stations and then maybe spending an hour at Seneca. Nothing can go wrong, you'll see.'

Ah, the optimism of youth! Were somebody to set out such a harebrained scheme as this to me now, I would just laugh and tell them to get out of here. When you get to this age, you just know that any human enterprise which relies upon one person passing themselves off as somebody else is certain-sure to miscarry. Well, I didn't see it then and neither did my brother. My mother should have stepped in and put a stop to it, which she could by just going down to the Pony Express stables and letting them know what was afoot. But, like I said, she too was hypnotized by that fifty dollars a month that we needed so badly. So, she did nothing, other than wringing her hands and making disapproving sounds.

Thursday 5 April dawned bright and clear, although with a hint of frost in the air, for all that it was spring. I was to be leaving the stable at seven in the morning sharp. One of the things that me and Jack had figured was that the later I got there, the better it would be. It would be much better to be in a mad hurry and not have time to be standing round chatting and allowing people to get a good look at me and perhaps starting to think to themselves something along the lines of: *Hmmm, that's a girlish sort of boy, with a high-pitched voice to boot. Something's not right here!*

Anyways, I went down to the centre of town and just kind of hung about near the stables until it lacked only five minutes to the hour of seven. Then I sauntered in casually and said as gruffly as I could manage, 'Taylor.'

The man I spoke to said angrily, 'Where the hell you been, boy? Wasn't you told to report here a full half-hour before seven? Never mind, you young

26

fellows is all limbs of Satan and that's a fact. Come now, your pony's all tacked up and rarin' to go.'

And with that he led me round to where a lively-looking little palomino was waiting. He said to a man standing near by, 'Where's that damned *mochila?*' It was handed to him and he slung it over the saddle and said irritably, 'Lord, what are you waiting for now? Just git goin', will you? See, the clock is about to strike the hour!'

With that I jumped up into the saddle and was away. Right up until that moment, I don't think that I really believed that our plan would come off and that I would be sent home with a flea in my ear. But no, there it was. I was racing off towards the ferry, where the steamboat was waiting 'til I was aboard before carrying me across the Missouri and depositing me on the opposite bank in Kansas. Once we touched the shore I was off again.

The way that things were arranged

was that there were stations every ten miles or so along the route, where a fresh horse was waiting, saddled up and ready to go. All that was needful was for me to jump off and let somebody take the *mochila* off this mount and transfer it to the next. The only consideration was speed and so there was no stopping for a chat or a cup of coffee and a smoke, nor anything of that nature. It was jump off, and then straight onto the next pony. I was to do that eight times between St Joseph and Seneca. Then, when once I reached Seneca. I would have time for a short rest and then take over on the eastward route; heading straight back the way I'd come.

William Russell had calculated that the average speed for journeys would be somewhere in the region of twelve and a half miles an hour, meaning that I would take a little over six hours to reach Seneca. Then there'd be an hour or so before I started back, meaning that I'd be in the saddle for about twelve hours in total that day. This was pretty gruelling, which was why the money was so good. Not that I minded at all, because I would a sight rather have been racing like the wind across open country on horseback, than I would staying at home and learning to cook or sew. There was no difficulty spotting where I was to change horses, because those locations had big signs over them, saying PONY EXPRESS. There's little enough to say about the ride to Seneca, for nothing much happened. I rode hard and fast and made it there a little after midday. And that was where things began to go wrong.

When I reined in at the station at Seneca I had been riding flat out, hell for leather for the better part of six hours. I had never undertaken a ride anything like so strenuous and the prospect of now carrying on for the same period of time again was a daunting one. Notwithstanding, I had little other choice, if me and my family were to gain that fifty dollars which meant so much to us. I knew that I would be allowed an hour's rest at Seneca, before starting back, and that was a blissful prospect.

The man in the yard greeted me by saying, 'Change o' plan son. We's a man down. You'll have to carry on west to Smoky Mountain.' My jaw must have dropped in dismay at the unwelcome announcement, because he continued sharply, 'An' you needn't look like that, neither. Don't get all antsy 'bout it, you knew when you signed up as you might have to carry on further west if need be.'

I managed to lower my voice a half-octave and growled, 'I get a break, though?'

The man softened then and said, 'Yeah, course you can have an hour's rest. Go over to the bunkhouse yonder and there's a pot o' coffee on the stove. Sorry 'bout all this here, it's just the way it is.'

I now faced a further ordeal, which was to walk into the exclusively masculine environment of the bunk-house and try to present myself as a young man. This promised to be a more taxing challenge than spending five and three-quarter hours in the saddle without a break, but there was nothing for it, so I strode over to the little building he had indicated and kicked open the door.

Luckily, I had been brought up with a brother who was just the very same age as me and so I had had many opportunities over the years to observe how boys did things. Jack would never open a door gently, but always barge through with his shoulder or kick it. I felt sure that I would be able to maintain this pretence for the hour or so that I would be there. By good fortune there was only one person in the place when I entered.

'Hiyah,' said a boy about the same age as me. 'You want some coffee?' He had a drawl, which made 'coffee' sound like 'cawfee'. It was an accent I did not recognize. I grunted an inarticulate reply and went over to the stove to pour myself a cup.

'They say as you're goin' on to Smoky Mountain. That right?'

Again, I made a vague, low sound in my throat which might equally well have signalled denial as it did assent. The youngster didn't seem to mind that I was seemingly not disposed to conversation, for he was one of those individuals who always have as much to say as two normal people. He was quite capable of keeping our exchange going under his own steam.

He said, 'Bet you was right surprised, when Bill told ya as you weren't goin' home now? I would o' been, I tell you that for naught!'

I shrugged and mumbled, 'I guess.'

'Lordy, you could o' knocked me down with a feather when Jimmy didn't show. They say as he's had to vanish for a spell. Caught thievin' is what I heard!'

Not knowing either Bill or Jimmy, made the conversation about these characters a little dull, but I was glad enough to lay back on a cot and listen. At least I was resting my . . . well that is to say that part of my anatomy that I had had planted in a saddle for nearly six hours!

'You hear what happen over Crooked Creekway?'

I shook my head and tried to show by my expression that I was raring to hear about the events in a corner of Kansas of which I had never even heard.

The boy said, 'Fellow come by here last night. Said as there'd been some big fight 'tween the cavalry and a bunch o' redskins. Wiped out the whole crew of 'em, seemingly. Soldiers killed too. Like a regular battle from what was told us.'

Since it has a direct bearing on what happened to me a few hours later, I guess I ought to explain what this was all about, as I found out later. For reasons which don't signify as far as my story's concerned, the Comanche were feeling a mite contentious about the white man just then. The army had come down on a group of fifty or sixty raiders at a little place called Crooked Creek and because there had been 600 cavalry facing fewer than a tenth of that number Indians; the result was not in doubt for a moment. They had disposed of one party of raiders, who had crossed into Kansas to pillage and loot, but didn't know until later that they had missed a far larger band, which consisted of several hundred warriors.

Of course, I didn't know any of this at the time and the boy's tales of some massacre, in a place I'd never heard of and wasn't likely ever to visit, didn't really interest me overmuch. You will scarcely credit it, but that young man carried on talking about this, that and nothing in particular for the whole hour I was there and I do not, to this very day, even know what his name was. Some folk are like that; enjoying the sound of their own voices so much that they forget about any of the social niceties.

The man whose name was apparently Bill came to tell me when it was time for me to leave.

He said, 'You just head straight east. You'll reach Smoky Mountain at seven or eight maybe and they'll give you a bunk for the night. You can take the road home again when the next eastbound rider hits there.' I nodded and grunted and then I was off again on my travels.

Now I can't recollect whether or not I have mentioned that I was carrying a pistol at my waist. This was a requirement for all the riders, and mine was a cap-and-ball revolver, the old Colt Navy model. This had belonged to my pa and, since it was the only gun our family owned, I had had to bring it with me. It surely came in handy, later on.

So there I was, racing across the country. I was tired, but the speed of the ride was exhilarating. Normally, when you are hacking out on a pony, the creature begins to flag after a space, but because I was changing mounts every ten or twelve miles there was none of this. The whole journey between those two stations was carried out at a gallop, with only occasional periods when I dropped to a canter. After I had changed my pony a half-dozen times since leaving Seneca, I was thinking that I was now on the home straight and that in another ten miles, maybe, I would be able to jump down and rest for the night. My mother used to say that: 'Man proposeth, but God disposeth' and so it proved on that evening, because by the time I reached the station at Smoky Mountain it was as plain as a pikestaff to me, even at such a tender age, that something was amiss.

I suppose that having at the back of my mind the name of the location, Smoky Mountain, had somehow acted upon my mind to condition me into expecting smoke, or something of the sort. At any rate, when I was, according to my calculations, only a mile or two from this Smoky Mountain, I suddenly realized that for some time past I had actually been able to smell smoke. When once I was aware of it, I began to wonder about it, because this smoke had the scent not merely of a campfire, but was mingled with a host of other, indefinable, smells.

I sniffed the air, and for some unknown reason didn't care at all for what I was smelling. There was little enough to be done about it for, good rider though I was, I was just about dead beat by then. I had been galloping with only a single break, for a little over twelve hours. Evening was coming on and I was just desirous of sliding down from my pony and flopping onto a bunk.

The track led through a wood and then the trees ended and there was a patch of scrubby grassland leading up a gentle slope to a ridge. I hoped that when I had mounted that ridge I might see the Smoky Mountain station on the other side and within easy reach. So I did, for all that it was worth.

As I gained the top of the ridge the smell of burning, which had been assailing my nostrils for the last few minutes, became an overpowering stench, and when I looked down to the plain which stretched before me the explanation was immediately obvious. There, smouldering in the evening air, with the sun about to dip below the distant horizon, was what remained of the Smoky Mountain station. It had, by the look of it, been put to the torch and left to burn to the ground. There was no sign of anybody in, near or about the place, which gave me to suppose that perhaps those who had been running it were dead or incapacitated. Even then, I don't think that it crossed my mind that all this was of any particular importance for me personally, or could have any implications for my future welfare. My only thought was that it was a damned shame that I would not, after all, be able to dismount and lie down on a soft bed.

I took the pony down at a leisurely walk, it being clear to me that there was not likely to be anybody at the station urging me on to hurry so that they could take the *mochila* from my mount in order speedily to transfer it to another. As I drew nigh to the ruins of what I supposed could only be the station a feeling of dread began to grip me. If there had been an accidental fire, then why had nobody troubled to extinguish it? Surely they could not all have been burned to death in their beds in such a case, so where was everyone? When I was maybe a couple of hundred yards away I halted and tried to make sense of the baffling circumstance which faced me. Although smoke was still trickling lazily up into the sky, it looked to me as though the fire had probably burned itself out hours earlier. All that remained were smouldering embers. I had seen the aftermath of fires before, but never until now had I witnessed the complete and utter destruction of any building by flames. Somebody always came and put out a fire before it reached that stage.

I started forward again and found that the pony was oddly reluctant to walk on. I urged him by squeezing my legs hard and then digging my heels sharply into his flanks and eventually he obeyed me. There was no doubt though that he was not happy about going any closer to the remains of the building. I jumped down and secured him to a stout sapling. Then I went over to see if there was any clue as to what had befallen the place. More than that, I was hoping for some indication of what my own next move should be. There was little purpose in staying here, but should I carry on to the next staging post, or return to the last?

I have said that the smell of wood smoke was mixed up with other, less familiar odours. One of these, now that I was a good deal closer, I identified as the faint, savoury tang of roasted meat, like somebody might have been having a barbecue. I discovered the source of this when I reached the doorway of the charred wreckage of the station. Laying half in what had once been the main building and partly in the yard outside, was the body of man. His legs and the lower half of his body had been almost wholly consumed by fire. Protruding from his upper body, lending him the startling appearance of a porcupine, were a dozen arrows. From the agonized look on his face, I would say that this unfortunate man most likely died hard, as the saying goes. I could not help but notice that the top of his head was one ghastly, bloody wound, where almost the whole of his scalp had been removed.

3

I had only ever seen one dead person before in the whole course of my young life. That had been my father and he had been tidied up by the mortician and arranged neatly in a pine coffin before I was allowed to view him. The man lying there, half-burned and bristling with war arrows, was something else again. I will freely own that I had nightmares about that corpse for a good long while after I saw it. When viewing my dead pa, you could have half-persuaded yourself that he was only sleeping and at any moment might open his eyes and announce that he was ready for his dinner. No such illusions were in any way possible with the man whose mortal remains lay on the ground at the Smoky Mountain Pony Express station.

I walked slowly round the stables, outbuildings and the rest of what had once been a station pretty much like the one at Seneca, from all that I was able to apprehend. I counted seven bodies, all of which had been scalped. My mind went back to what the boy at Seneca had said about the fight with the Indians and it struck me that this carnage was perhaps part and parcel of the same affair. Five of the bodies had arrows in them; the other two, judging by the huge pools of congealed blood surrounding them and the wounds on their necks, had died after having their throats cut.

I felt sick at the sight and smell of so much butchery and blood and I stumbled off to a little copse near the burned-out station in order to empty my stomach. I had snatched a few handfuls of parched corn and also a little dried meat which my mother had given me but, that apart, I had eaten nothing since breaking my fast that morning. Nevertheless, I felt my gorge rising and knew that I should vomit in another few seconds. Why I felt that I had to seek the privacy of the little stand of trees in order to throw up, I don't rightly know. There was, after all, not a living soul to see me. Howsoever, that is what I did. It was when I reached the clump of birches and was leaning over and preparing to hasten matters by poking my fingers down my throat, that I heard somebody say, in a low voice, 'Hey, boy!'

Having convinced myself that I was surrounded only by dead men, you may perhaps guess what a shock I received when I heard somebody speaking to me out loud. I thought that my heart would have stopped beating, such was the terror I felt. I forgot about vomiting and looked around fearfully, fully expecting to see a dead man tottering towards me. I had not yet grown out of fearing the bogie man, you see. Then the voice spoke again, this time with a hint of impatience. Well, I had never in my life heard of an impatient or irritable corpse and so this reassured me.

'Never mind those that are dead,' said the voice, 'Tend to me now!'

I looked round and soon saw what I had missed before. A dreadfully injured man was somehow concealed within the thicket that surrounded the base of the trees. He was wearing a buckskin jacket and had long, greasy, grey hair, which was tied back like a girl's. His face and clothing were liberally besmeared with blood and there was a jagged, raw cut across his face, like he might have been slashed with a knife or sword.

'I'm sorry,' I said. 'I didn't see you there.'

'Never mind the chat. We don't have long.'

I looked at him in the fading light and although I had never seen a dying person, it struck me most forcefully that here was a man who was not long for this world.

I said, 'Can I do anything for you, sir?'

'Yes,' he replied in a thin but vigorous tone, as though he were used to people doing as he bid. 'You can stop talking and listen to what I say. Come closer. I'm failing fast.'

I crouched down at the man's head. Up close, he looked older than you would have guessed from his voice. I would say that he must have been closer to sixty than fifty. He gazed up at me and said, 'You look awful young. How old are you?'

'I'm fifteen years of age.'

'Why, you're no more than a baby!' The man tried to smile as he said this, but it turned to a grimace of pain. He continued: 'Whether or no, I reckon you'll have to do. I heard you ride up. You're from the express?'

'I am. Are you sure I can't fetch you my canteen or something?'

'In a minute. Listen up, now. It was Comanches done this. They're on the rampage, good and proper. I don't belong here. I'm a scout.' He stopped speaking for a bit, as though to gather

46

his strength. Then he said, 'All the others dead?'

'Yes, sir.'

'Then it falls to you.'

I didn't like the sound of this one little bit. I had had enough of adventures now to last me a good long while and the only thing on my mind was how to get back to my mother in St Joseph.

I said, 'I got to deliver the mail. That's my job.'

'Damn your mail, you young fool. There's lives at stake here. Women and children, well as men. You do as I say, now. You know the way to Fort Richmond from here?'

'I never heard of it. I ain't from these parts.'

'It's forty miles north o' here. Army base. You got to get word to 'em. Tell 'em what's happened here. Nobody knows as those Indians are crossing into Kansas in force from the Indian Nations. More'n you could guess. You understand?'

I was almost in tears at the unfairness

of it all. All this, riding with the Pony Express and all, had only been meant as a lark; a kind of childhood escapade which had the great advantage of getting my family out of a hole and saving us from losing our home. I should by now have been back in St Joseph, excitedly recounting to my mother and brother how nobody had known that I was girl and that we had pulled the wool over their eyes good and proper.

Instead, I was stranded out here, over 150 miles from home, surrounded by mutilated corpses and with a dying man giving me an urgent commission to ride alone to some army camp I'd never heard of.

'There's more to it than that, son.' said the scout, who, even as I watched, looked to me to be growing weaker and paler. The effort of so much talking seemed to be exhausting him. ' 'Tween here and Fort Richmond there's a little settlement. Ever hear o' New Jerusalem?' I shook my head dumbly. 'They're religious types, Quakers or some such. Some of 'em are lately come from England. They built a town, want to live God-fearing lives away from other folk. Well, they're right in the path of the storm, as you might say.'

'I never even heard of these folk,' I said and now the tears were really beginning to start from my eyes. It was partly the delayed shock of seeing and smelling those dead men and also the way things had miscarried for me, but I was, to put the case plainly, frightened out of my wits at the predicament in which I found myself. The scout saw my eyes sparkling and the sight seemed to enrage him. He mustered his strength and said fiercely, 'This ain't a time to start bawling like a child. You hear what I say? You got to be a man.' Even at the time, in the midst of my distress, the irony of this statement did not escape me.

'What would you have me do?' I asked in desperation.

'Good boy. You got to ride hard as

the wind to New Jerusalem. Those folk don't even carry iron, they thinks as guns is sinful. They gonna be slaughtered if the Comanches descend on 'em. You got to get them to go for refuge north to Fort Richmond. Then you got to ride to the fort and tell the cavalry what's what. Think you can do it?'

'Yes, sir. I'll surely try.'

'Good man. Now I could do with a draught from that canteen as you mentioned earlier.'

The sun had now sunk completely below the horizon; it would not be long before darkness fell. As I went over to my pony to fetch the canteen it suddenly dawned on me that I did not have so much as a blanket to huddle in for the night. I began to shiver in fear and then stopped myself by a conscious effort of will. I thought about the mocking and unkind things that my brother would have said, if ever he heard of such a thing. It would confirm all the silly views that he held, or purported to hold, about girls in general and me in particular.

When I returned with the water to the wounded scout, his eyes were closed and I could not see any sign of his breathing. For a terrible moment I thought that he had died and that I was now altogether alone with a bunch of dead men. At that moment he opened his eyes and appeared somehow to divine what had been in my thoughts, for he said, 'Don't be affeared, I ain't dead yet!'

After he had taken a long gulping drink from the canteen, the man handed it back to me, saying, 'Well, what are you waiting for? You got a job o' work to undertake.'

I looked at him blankly and replied, 'Oh, but I can't leave you here alone.'

He laughed at that, the sound coming out more like a bark than anything one would associate with mirth or amusement. He said, 'I'll do well enough. Get goin'. If you don't persuade them folk in Jerusalem to go for refuge, then they'll be killed, every man Jack of 'em.'

I am ashamed to admit it, but my reluctance to leave the gravely injured man was actuated less by compassion on my part for him, than by a fear for my own self of riding alone through the dark in an area which was apparently full of hostile Indians. In a gentler voice than he had hitherto used, the man said, 'Don't you worry 'bout me. Just do your duty now. I'm dying, case you ain't noticed. I want to be alone to meet my maker. I have to make my peace with him while I'm still able.'

'Would you like me to . . . I don't know . . . say a prayer or aught?'

'There's no time for such foolishness, though I'm thankful for the offer. Me and the Lord need to speak man to man and we don't neither of us need any witnesses. Off you go now.'

'I just head north, is that right?'

'You got it.'

I reached out and grasped the man's hand, which was grimy and sticky with blood. I said, 'I hope that you get right with the Lord.'

'Him and me haven't had much dealings lately. We'll take it as it comes. Get going.'

So it was that I went back to the pony, mounted and then went trotting off into the darkening evening.

I might add at this point that I never did learn that man's name, nor discover what he was doing in that thicket. Whether he was with the army or had some connection with the Pony Express, I couldn't say. I read later in the newspapers that eight bodies had been found at the burned-out remains of the Smoky Mountain station and I guess one of the corpses must have been his.

The night was crisp and cool, with the promise of a frost the next morning. I was dog-tired and knew that if I didn't snatch some sleep, then I would end up passing out on the back of my horse. I surely could have done with a blanket or something to wrap myself in, but since I had nothing of the sort there was no use fretting over it. I found a sheltered spot, off the track and shielded from the wind by a clutch of boulders. There, I untacked the pony and tethered him near at hand before trying to arrange myself for sleep.

It was no easy task to sleep fully clothed, out in the open on a chilly night like that. So tired was I, though, that I fell asleep fairly swiftly, notwithstanding the unfavourable conditions. The night was restless and uneasy though. I was constantly being woken by strange scurrying noises, as of animals near at hand. Once or twice I heard a snuffling; like a bigger animal was close. This caused my heart to race, in case it was a bear, wolf or some other animal that might do me harm. Despite all this I succeeded in getting a few hours of sleep before the dawn came and I found myself drenched through with the morning dew.

It was a miserable and wretched morning and I was feeling thoroughly dispirited and sorry for myself. I had a few pieces of dried meat left for breakfast, and these I washed down with swigs of water. Then I thought that I might as well be on the move as sitting around moping. Besides which, from all that I was able to gather, there really were some poor folks in danger and if that scout had spoken truly, then it depended altogether upon me to help them to safety.

The day looked as though it might be a fine one and I thought it wise to make as much speed as ever I could. This Fort Richmond was supposedly forty miles away, and so the town I had been told of must be something less than that. With a steady pace I was hopeful of reaching it before midday. I would need to pace the pony carefully; there was no question of pushing him the way I had yesterday, when a fresh mount was no more than twelve miles ahead of me. For all I knew to the contrary, this pony would have to see me safely over the next forty miles, and if I somehow lamed him then it was all up, not only with me but also with those helpless people with the Comanches bearing down on them.

I knew that the track I was following headed directly north, but whether it would lead to this New Jerusalem place of which I had been told, was more than I could say. At every touch and turn I was expecting some bloodthirsty savage to leap out at me from behind a tree, and so when I saw two riders in the distance, heading towards me, I was initially nervous and tempted to ride off the track and try and hide in the nearby woods. Before I had reached a decision we were close enough for me to see that, rather than being Indian braves, they were just a pair of travel-stained white men. Feeling reassured and thinking that I could do worse than ask them for directions to this New Jerusalem, I carried on until I was within hailing distance.

Now although I had at first been relieved to find that these were not

Comanches who might be planning to scalp me, I found that as I got close enough to examine the men carefully I did not care at all for the look of them. It was not so much that they looked dirty and rough. I looked pretty beat-up myself after the previous day's hard riding, followed by a night spent sleeping in my clothes.

No, it was the expression on their faces that made me uneasy. They looked cunning and mean. It was too late to avoid the meeting, though, because they were watching me closely. I could see that they were also discussing me as they came on and this too raised my hackles.

When they were twenty feet away the men reined in and one said, 'Hidy, fellow. Where you headed?'

Although I had at first thought of asking for directions, now that I could see them plainly the last thing I intended was to let them know where I was going, and so I said, 'Nowhere special.'

The other one said in a low, ugly voice, 'Don't you dare sass me, boy. My partner here asked you a question. You just give him a civil answer.'

'I'm going north.'

'Where you come from? You runnin' away?'

I shrugged. I was starting to feel alarmed, because these men didn't look like they were going to let me pass for some reason. There were in those days various scamps around who preyed on travellers, robbing and sometimes killing them. Occasionally, they went after bigger game, taking down mail coaches or even trains. Some called these types 'road agents' and I was afraid that these men were of that brand. They weren't common near big towns like St Joseph, but in wild country like this there was less law and order.

During this brief exchange the two riders had started turning their horses sideways to me, so that it would be no easy task to ride on past them. Both were wearing guns and I had an uncomfortable notion that they might be accustomed to using them. The one who had first spoken to me looked to be about twenty-five years of age, and the other perhaps thirty or so.

The younger man said, 'You know what we want. You best get down and let us take your horse, else you're apt to get hurt.'

Hearing this, a rage began to flood through me: a seething anger such as I had never before felt in my life. This fury was mingled with and sharpened by great fear. There was a coppery taste in my mouth; like I had been sucking coins or something. I was more afraid than I had ever been in my life before. At the same time I knew that I wasn't about to let these rascals take my pony. All else apart, there were people's lives at stake, other than mine. On the other hand, it would be dangerous to let them know at once that I wasn't going to cooperate.

I said, 'What would you have me do?'

'That's the sensible dodge,' said the

59

older man, 'Lucky for you, you're one of the smart ones. Get down from the pony. Nice and slowly.'

Because of the way that the *mochila* rucked up in the front, they hadn't had a clear view below my waist and so did not know that I was carrying a pistol. I made sure that as I twisted round meekly to dismount they didn't catch sight of the holster hanging from my belt. I got down on the side away from them.

Once I was down, the two men turned their horses and walked on towards me and my pony. At this point I drew the pistol, cocking it with my thumb as I did so. I was more frightened than I had ever before been in my life, but I was not about to give up on the important commission which had been entrusted to me.

'Now step clear of your horse,' said the younger of the men. He was almost affable, thinking that he and his partner had got what they wanted without any trouble. His face changed with astonishing rapidity when I walked out from behind the pony with a gun in my hand, which was aimed in their direction.

'What are you about?' asked the older of the two, and I was pleased to remark that his voice had risen a little in alarm. Perhaps it was a novelty for him to have somebody draw down on him.

'You ain't taking this horse,' I said. 'Try it and I'll shoot you both.'

Both of them looked stumped and puzzled as to how to deal with this sudden turnabout in fortune. The young man said, 'Put up your weapon and we'll talk.'

'Got nothing to say to you. It's my horse.'

I have no bad conscience about what happened next, because they could just have ridden on and left me alone. As it was, the older man ran out of patience and did not perhaps take overmuch to a boy of my age pointing a gun at him. Perhaps he thought that I was bluffing and, being so young and green, would not follow through on my threat.

Ignoring me, he urged on his horse and made a grab for my pony's bridle, meaning to take him from me and leave me on foot. I had already taken first pull on the trigger and, at the sight of a thief making off with my horse, I did what anybody might have done under the given circumstances. I shot him.

4

The crash of gunfire seemed shockingly loud, partly perhaps because it was so sudden and unexpected. I don't believe either me or those two men had believed for a moment that there was going to be shooting. The man I had shot sat there for a fraction of a second and then began twitching and convulsing, following which he pitched sideways and fell from his horse, although one foot remained entangled in the stirrup.

The dead man's partner stared uncomprehendingly at the scene for a moment, hardly able to credit the evidence of his senses. Then he looked at me and began fumbling frantically for his own pistol. If that first shot had been a surprise, even to me, the second was not. I knew that unless I acted swiftly, the man now going for his gun would kill me. I cocked my piece and fired again, catching the other road agent in his chest, slightly to one side. He stopped trying to draw and looked down at the wound I had given him.

Then he said, 'I never thought you'd shoot us. To be bested by a boy!'

'It's worse than that,' I told him. 'I ain't even a boy. I'm a girl.'

The fellow stared stupidly at me and then kind of hiccuped or burped. As he did so, a bubble of crimson appeared on his lips. Then he too slumped, unconscious, although instead of falling sideways he collapsed forward and so remained on his horse.

I recall being vaguely taken aback that none of the three horses seemed to have been spooked by the gunfire. Maybe they were used to it; I couldn't say. At any rate, the little tableau remained intact for a spell. I stood there with my gun in my hand and the two men whom I had shot, as one might expect, stayed just right where they were. I suppose that, being dead, this was not to be wondered at.

Grown-up people view death with reverence and amazement. It is generally thought to be a fearful thing to end the life of another human being. Young people, though, are in many ways harder and more careless in affairs of that kind. Death is not a matter of such consequence to them and they are sometimes more apt to take it in their course.

So it was with me. So great had been my fear of those two rogues that my strongest and most immediate feeling was one of enormous relief that they were no longer a threat to me. Later on I was pretty disturbed about what I had done, but just then I couldn't see what other choice I had had. At the back of my mind I had perhaps sensed that even giving them my horse might not have been enough to save me, and that they could have killed me anyway, simply to dispose of a dangerous witness.

Anyway, I was now breathing a little

65

easier in the knowledge that I was still able to undertake the duty which had been laid upon me by a dying man. There are those who will find my next action shocking, but it didn't strike me so at the time. I was ravenously hungry and thought that if I didn't soon eat something a little more nourishing and sustaining than parched corn, then I might end up fainting. The upshot was that I decided to look through the dead men's saddlebags for anything in the way of vittles.

In the event it was only needful to look in one pack, because there I found rolls, cheese and a half-haunch of the juiciest and most succulent ham that you ever saw in your life. My mouth began to water as soon as I set eyes upon these delicacies. I hastily snatched them up and then led my pony away from the two corpses, where I made a good breakfast. This too is an instance of the callousness and want of natural feeling that afflicts so many young people. You might have thought that killing two men would have put me off my food, but nothing of the sort.

Now in those days Kansas was, to say the least of it, pretty sparsely inhabited. I rode for another hour before seeing any signs of human life. This consisted of a few cultivated fields, beyond which I could see a little log cabin. Since I was desirous of making sure that the track I was on would lead me in due season to Fort Richmond, I thought it prudent to stop and check with one of the locals who might know more of the matter than I did myself. Accordingly, I turned from the track and began heading towards the little farm. I was destined never to reach it, though, because no sooner had I reached the fields surrounding the wooden house than there was the dull boom of a scattergun being discharged.

I at once reined in, but could neither see nor hear anything to indicate who had fired the shot. It was entirely possible that whoever had used that shotgun was hunting wildfowl or something, and it had been nothing to do with me. After the events of the last twelve hours or so, though, I guess my nerves were twisted tight to breaking point and so I just turned tail and cantered back in the direction from which I had come.

The firing of a scattergun near at hand had made me more edgy than had my encounter with the two road agents. You can most generally deal, in one way or another, with those who confront you on the highway. A concealed man with a twelve-gauge shotgun is something else entirely.

I rode on for half an hour more and then came to what looked to be a little hamlet, consisting of three soddies and two buildings constructed of logs. I could hear the clang of a hammer striking iron and it occurred to me that maybe a blacksmith or farrier was at work. This promised well and so I cantered on towards the buildings.

I had been right about the source of the sounds, for a tall, brawny-looking fellow was swinging a hammer at an anvil. When he caught sight of me approaching he set down the hammer, wiped his hands on the leather apron which he was wearing and walked towards me, a cheerful and welcoming smile on his face. When he was close enough not to need to raise his voice, he said, 'Well, you're a young enough pilgrim to be on the road alone! Where you bound for?'

There was something so open and good-natured about his countenance that I did not hesitate for a moment, but said straight out, 'I'm looking first for a town called New Jerusalem and then after that an army base called Fort Richmond.'

He looked at me thoughtfully and said, 'Seems to me there's a story needs telling here. I can set you on the right path easy enough, but have you time to stop for a taste of cold milk?'

After having drunk nothing other than water for the last twenty-four hours a glass of milk sounded fine and so I said, 'Yes, please. But I can't stop long. I have urgent business.'

'Urgent business, is it? You're powerful young to be engaged upon 'urgent business'. But anyways, come with me to the house.'

Although I was in a hurry, the idea of talking to somebody who wasn't either dying or set on robbing me was a pleasant one and I was beginning to feel the after-effects of having been involved in that little episode of gunplay earlier. Leaving my pony to feed, I suffered the man to lead me into the kitchen of the largest of the wood-framed buildings. A woman was at work there, churning butter from what I could see.

The man said, 'My dear, this young man could do with a drink of cold milk.'

The woman, who was about the same age as the man, in her forties perhaps, gave me a shrewd look and then laughed. She said, 'Your wits aren't as sharp as once they were, Jethro. Either that or your eyesight's failing. This isn't a young man, it's a girl-child.'

The man stared hard at me and then said, 'Bless me if you're not right, Martha. This is a rum go and no mistake! What's the meaning of it, young fellow — I mean lady?'

'What's your name, honey?' asked the woman.

'I'm Beth Taylor.'

'Well, Beth Taylor, just set yourself at the table and tell us what's going on.'

'I can't stay long, I have to take word to Fort Richmond, north of here.'

The woman and the man I now took to be her husband exchanged looks, and then she said, 'Tell us what this is about, child. Mayhap we can aid you.'

So it was that I consented to sit at the table with a mug of foaming, creamy milk and gave them a brief account of the last few days of my recent life. I left out the shooting of the two men, feeling that this wasn't a subject to bandy about. When I had finished, the man called Jethro shook his head and said, 'Lord a mercy, I never heard the like!'

Then he grew very serious and said, 'You say that there's a great number of Comanches now crossed into this territory from the Indian Nations?'

'So I took it from what I was told.'

'Martha,' said Jethro, 'Call in those boys of ours from the fields. This wants thinking on.'

She whom I took to be his wife stood up and then left the house in something of a hurry.

'Have you ate lately?' asked the man.

'Yes, I thank you.'

'I see you're carrying a gun. Know how to use it?'

'Yes,' I replied in a hard, tight voice, 'I should just about say as I do.' Jethro looked at me oddly, and for a moment it seemed as though he were about to speak further. Then he gave an all but imperceptible shrug and remained silent. The woman called Martha returned with three tall, handsome young men, all of whom looked to be around the age of twenty or so.

'These three useless articles are our

sons,' said their mother, with an air of obvious and undisguised pride, 'From the left, there's Ezra, Caleb and Joshua.'

The three boys looked as merry and high-spirited as you like, putting me in mind of my own brother. You had the feeling that life around these fellows would never be dull.

'This here is Beth,' continued their mother, 'and she's travelling on from here to take a message to some folks.'

Jethro interrupted at this point and said, 'If what this girl says is right, we're all of us in danger. Ezra, you and Caleb break out our musketry and powder. I reckon the four of us should be able to hold off any number of Indians from in here, should it come to it. Martha, my dear, perhaps you would start putting up the shutters. There's loopholes enough for firing, should it come to it.'

I was amazed to hear the matter-of-fact way that this man gave directions for preparing for a siege, but I suppose that, living as they did in such wild country and so close to the Indian

Nations, this wasn't the first such alarm they had had.

'What about me, Pa?' asked one of his sons. 'What shall I do?'

'Here's the way of it, son,' said his father, 'We needs must give the warning to our neighbours. They'd undertake the same office for us, if things were reversed. This young lady is riding to Fort Richmond to call on the army for help, seeing as they don't yet know of this. She's going to that set of Quakers first, over by the three falls. I thought that you and she could ride along of each other.'

'I hate to leave you and Ma here — ' began the young man, but his father cut him off, firmly but definitely.

'Would you like to hear it said later that we let a young girl, not yet sixteen years of age, carry the warning alone and fetch aid for us?'

At that, Joshua looked a mite shamefaced and said, 'No, I guess not. You're in the right, Pa. I'll do it.' He turned to me and then thrust out his hand, grinning in an engaging way. 'My name's Joshua and yourn is Beth, right?'

I smiled shyly and said, 'Yes, that's right.'

'Well, well,' said his father impatiently. 'Get to and saddle up, son.' Turning to me, he said, 'We're mighty grateful that you've brung us word of this hazard, Miss Taylor. I hope we'll meet again.'

Joshua's mother came over and embraced me, saying, 'Are you sure you don't want to stay here with us, my dear? I'll warrant that son of mine is well able to spread word of this all the way clear up to Fort Richmond.'

'It's right kind of you ma'am, but I promised that scout that I'd do this my own self. I wouldn't feel good about being faithless in an oath to a dying man.'

'The girl's right, Martha,' said her husband. 'She's honourable and true. Now let them depart, or it'll be too late.'

So it was that Joshua and I rode off from the farm where he and his family lived, and headed north along the way that would lead us to New Jerusalem.

I was glad indeed to have a travelling companion and this young fellow seemed to be a pleasant boy. Because I'd grown up with a brother of the same age, whom I was very close to, I never felt any awkwardness about being in the company of young men. Some of the girls I knew of my age in St Joseph simpered, blushed and giggled if a boy so much as bid them good day. I was never like that and enjoyed being with boys of my own age every bit as much as I did girls. This Joshua sensed that I wasn't the giggling type of coquettish miss, and he was soon chatting away to me as though we'd known each other all our lives.

'What's this town, this New Jerusalem, like?' I asked.

'It's a real nice location. All the folk there live like one big family. They share everything and all the people look out for one another.'

'They pious?' Many of the religious types that I had in the past encountered had been self-righteous hypocrites and I guess that I had it in mind to wonder what a whole town full of such people would be like. It was not, from what I had known of 'religious' people, an attractive prospect.

Joshua wrinkled his forehead and said, 'I suppose you could call them pious, yes. But not in a stuffy, holy way. They're just good folk who are right with the Lord and watch out for each other.'

'How far might it be to there?'

'Maybe fifteen miles, a bit more perhaps. I never calculated. We have to stop off at a few farms on the way, if that's all right with you. We all spread word of any trouble like this and whoever first hears tells his neighbours.'

As we rode Joshua talked of his life on his father's farm and I in turn told him about living in St Joseph. He was struck speechless to hear that I had ridden for the new Pony Express and after I had talked of that and finding the station at Smoky Mountain burned out, I found that he kept looking at me sideways, as if I were some sort of oddity or freak. When he became aware that I had caught him doing this, he flushed slightly and said, 'I don't mean to stare, but I never did meet a girl like you in my life. You got more grit than most boys.'

I laughed at that and said, 'My brother and me, we did the same things as each other when we were growing up. Riding, shooting, wrestling. You name it, I can do it.'

'See you're carrying. Can you fire that pistol straight?'

Now I hadn't felt like telling the story to grown people like his parents, but Joshua wasn't more than a few years older than me, which meant I felt more at ease with him. I told him how I had shot the two men who had attempted to deprive me of my horse. When I had finished the tale, he said nothing for a few seconds and then exclaimed, 'God almighty! I never heard the like. You are the beatenest girl I ever did set eyes on.'

I was extremely proud to hear Joshua say this and rode along afterwards with a pleasurable feeling.

The first farm we stopped at was a mean and poky little place, which looked to me more like a pigpen than anywhere that human beings might inhabit.

'This here's the O'Learys' home,' said Joshua, 'They struggle hard, but never seem to get on overmuch.'

He delivered the warning of the Indian incursion into the territory and we were neither invited to stay, nor indeeed did Joshua show any inclination to do so. After we had travelled on for a bit, he abruptly announced, 'They really are a shiftless bunch. We're always helping them out in different ways. Old Mick O'Leary, he's a moonshiner. Drinks as much as he sells of the poteen, far as I can make out.'

'If we carry on straight along this

track, will that bring us to New Jerusalem?'

'No, when we reach a river, five miles from here, this track starts going to the right. To get to Jerusalem you need to veer to the left a mite. There's no track at first, but if you keep going for a space, you come upon it.'

'What about this Fort Richmond? Is the road to that easy to find after you leave Jerusalem?'

'Yes, it's a straight road from there, all the way to the fort.'

The next little homestead at which we called was a good deal more pleasant than that of the O'Learys. It was a bright, two-storey wooden house, encircled by neat and well-tended fields. Alongside the house was a little vegetable garden.

I remarked, 'This is sweet.'

'Friend of mine lives here,' said Joshua, looking bashful. 'Real good friend.'

There was a woman working at the back of the house, and when she saw us coming she waved. Once we were near enough she said cheerfully, 'If you're looking for that daughter of mine, Joshua, your luck's out. Ellie-May has gone visiting with her father.'

When Joshua had apprised her of the real reason for our visit the woman went pale and said, 'Lord, you don't say so? You saw no sign of marauders on your way here?'

'Not a bit of it ma'am, but you'd best stay in the house. You have weapons to hand?'

'I got a musket,' she said grimly, 'Know how to use it too. Well, I'll bid you good day and I'll make sure to pass your greeting on to Ellie-May.'

As we left I began chaffing Joshua gently about this Ellie-May. He took it in good part and I found that I could talk as free and easy to this good humoured farm boy as I could to my own brother. In the short time that we had known each other, I think that I had the measure of him and I was glad of the instinct which had led me to his door. It surely was more agreeable to ride along like this with a companion who knew the area, rather than wander about, hoping for the best. Our mission might have been a deadly serious one, but we were also two youngsters out riding — on a fine April morning as well — and there was something pleasurably exciting about what were doing. It made me feel real grown up.

We were alternately trotting and cantering, there being need to travel fast but, because the distance was fairly great, there was no purpose in wearing out our animals. I had the impression that Joshua was trying to see how good a rider I really was, because from time to time when we were trotting along at a fairly sedate pace, he would suddenly spur on his horse and forge ahead. I was able to catch him up almost immediately and I suppose that this became a kind of game between us as we journeyed on.

Our way took us past scrubby grassland interspersed here and there with homesteads. I asked if Joshua was going to call at each and every one of them, but he said that would not be necessary. Word would soon be spread from the few that he did favour with a visit.

It must have been approaching midday when we came to the river that he had told me of, where the track went to the right, and we had to head left. There were woods along the side of the track here, stretching off to our right and leading up into some hills. We reined in at the ford and surveyed the scene. Everything was as peaceful as could be. The river was little more than a large stream; it would not be difficult to cross. I turned to Joshua and said, 'It's real pretty round here.'

He smiled and took breath to answer, but before he could do so there was a sound like a woodpecker striking a tree trunk and almost at once, from the front of the young man's throat, an arrowhead protruded, having evidently been driven through from behind. As it emerged from his throat, a few drops of blood were sprayed over me. Then there was a whoop of triumph and from the trees emerged three men on horseback. I didn't know a whole heap about Indians, but I was inclined to believe that these must be Comanches.

5

Now there are maybe those who will be shocked to hear what course of action I next pursued. They will probably be people who have never faced imminent death from a bunch of bloodthirsty hostiles or been entrusted with a task which might ensure the safety of hundreds of innocent men, women and children.

Joshua was making choking noises, like he might have something stuck in his throat; which, on reflection, was undoubtedly the case. He was shaking and attempting to cough and you didn't have to be a doctor to tell that he was as good as dead that very minute. For my own part, I was keenly aware of the three Indians who had now set their ponies trotting in my direction; so, without further ado, I wheeled round and set off across the river at a brisk canter.

When they saw that I might be about to escape their clutches, the Comanche braves let out a series of spine-chilling, warbling cries and set off in pursuit of me. I knew then that, if ever there had been a matter of life or death, this ride was it.

Now my pony had had to work hard over the last day or so: no question about that. Still and all, he was a hardy little beast and he made a valiant effort under my frantic urging to outpace the Comanches. It was fairly plain to me, though, that this was a hopeless enterprise. A quick glance back showed me that the gap between us was slowly but inexorably shrinking.

I considered briefly the wisdom of turning round in the saddle and trying to fire at the men chasing me. I was, as you will recall, a tolerably fair to middling shot with a pistol. However, although that sort of performance might be all well and good for a Wild West show, in real life it is a non-starter.

The most likely consequence would be not only missing my target by twenty yards, but also losing control of my mount and taking a tumble. When you're galloping at full pelt, the very last thing you should contemplate doing is ending up peering in the opposite direction to that in which you are travelling!

Of course, there was another side to the coin when thinking about firing at each other, which was that the men who were after me laboured under a precisely similar handicap. At one point, I was vaguely aware of a blur of movement to my right and glanced round anxiously, in case one of the riders was on the point of outflanking me. In fact, one of them must have loosed off an arrow while they were galloping at full speed. It came no closer to me than thirty or forty feet and they did not seemingly feel inclined to waste any more arrows in that way.

Another look behind me revealed that the gap between us was now no more than twenty yards or so. We were racing on the flat, across springy turf, and if it had not been such a desperate business, then this might have been an enjoyable gallop. When I heard a shot my heart leaped into my throat and I imagined that the men behind me were throwing caution to the wind and firing after me.

I had not been paying much attention to my surroundings, putting every fibre of my being into outrunning the men who surely meant me harm, but after the shot I noticed a slight movement ahead of me and to my left. When I looked I saw that it was a puff of smoke spreading out and that this had been produced by two men, who were aiming rifles at either me or the men behind me.

The question of who were their targets was settled when there was another puff of smoke, followed by the crack of a shot. I risked a quick look behind me and saw, to my immense relief, that two of the Indians had been shot from their horses. The third had reined in and was evidently giving up the chase.

The overwhelming feeling of joy, that I was not after all about to be butchered by Indians, was combined with a feeling of gratitude to the men who had been my saviours. I felt that it would be churlish not to at least thank them for what they had done, despite my great hurry. I slowed down to a trot and guided my pony over to where the two of them were standing, their weaponry lowered, looking thoughtfully at me as I came on. When I reached the men, I said, 'I'm right grateful for what you done. I don't know what would have become of me otherwise.'

The two men looked lean, rangy types: hard as nails and perhaps not overly given to needless chat. One of them said to me, 'Couldn't leave you to be killed.'

'Well, thank you.' I thought that I should spread the word as widely as possible about the incursion from the

Indian Nations and so I continued, 'There's a whole bunch of Comanches heading this way. From all I've been told, it's a regular invasion.'

The man who had not yet spoken, said, 'I counted three and two of them's dead now. I don't call that much of an invasion.' His friend smiled at this.

'Well, I have to ride to Fort Richmond to send word to the cavalry there,' I said, a little put out that my momentous news was being received so casually, 'Am I on the right track?'

'Surely. Just carry on north.'

'I need first to reach somewhere called New Jerusalem. Is that this way as well?'

'Keep on straight and you'll soon find it.'

'Well, good day to you both and thank you again.'

The two of them nodded at me amiably enough, but they both had faintly puzzled expressions on their faces, like they couldn't make out the play. I think now that I had been so excited by the chase and all, that I hadn't remembered to lower my voice at all and they had guessed that despite my clothing and hair; I was really a girl. That would have been enough to cause anybody to look puzzled.

Anyway, I had been freed from the imminent fear of death and that was something to be glad about. Now that I was no longer in such dreadful peril, though, I fell to thinking about Joshua. I had only known him for an exceedingly short time, but what I had seen of him had impressed me favourably. I was sorry that my very last memory of the boy would forever be that arrow jutting out from the front of his throat. I could only hope that he had died quickly.

I hope that I won't be thought hardhearted by anybody for the seemingly off-hand way that I talk about the deaths of others, but I was most keenly aware the whole time that I had a mission to undertake; one which was quite literally a matter of life and death.

It was this which fully occupied my thoughts as I rode, leaving little space for private griefs.

I gained the town which I had been seeking since I had left Smoky Mountain the previous day, just a half-hour after being freed from the pursuit of the Indians. I say town, but that is perhaps too grand a word for what I found when once I had picked up the track north again.

The settlement which I stumbled upon consisted of around twenty or thirty dwellings, most of which were set up in a line, as though to suggest a street. Some were stout, wooden-framed structures, but most were soddies. Maybe, for those who are unfamiliar with the term, I should explain what I mean by 'soddies'.

In some parts of the developing territories at that time, there were plenty of trees, which meant that you could chop a few down and make a little log cabin. Elsewhere, there was only grassland; this presented a greater problem when it came to building a house. The problem was solved by constructing what were, in essence, no more than glorified mud huts. Blocks of turf were dug up and then piled one on top of the other to make walls. These could then be roofed over with tar-paper or some other waterproof material. This then was a soddy and they were very popular with many homesteaders. Some were quite elaborate affairs and they could even, with a little ingenuity, be made into two-storey houses.

Some of the dwellings that made up the so-called 'town' of New Jerusalem were no more than one room, adobe shacks. Others were larger and had second floors. In addition to the soddies and handful of wooden houses and barns, there was a well-built wooden church, which appeared to be the focal point of the whole settlement. As I rode in I could see no sign of any store or saloon though, which might perhaps have been a sign of their Godliness.

There weren't all that many folk around, but those I did see were dressed modestly in dark and sober clothes. You got the feeling that these were people who took life seriously. Despite what more than one person had told me about these being Quakers, they were nothing of the sort. Instead, they belonged to some altogether harsher and more religiously observant sect, more akin to Hutterites than anything else.

My arrival in what I suppose might be called their main street caused no little consternation. Two women who were walking by with little children gathered their charges anxiously to them, as though I might be planning to make off with them. A man stopped dead in his tracks and stared openly at me, as if I was the strangest creature he ever had set eyes upon.

Now it was at this point that I encountered a problem which I am sure has long since struck those reading this. It is that it is all well and good for folk to say, 'Go and warn those in such and such town, tell them they must leave their homes at once.' Unless, though, you happen to be like some prophet of olden times, whose words will be heeded by all those who hear them, then actually carrying out this task is apt to be at best embarrassing and at worst, utterly useless. When you are a dusty, dishevelled young girl who is trying to pass herself of as a boy, then this is likely to be an even trickier business. I said to the man who was gaping at me, 'There's a whole heap of Comanches heading this way. You and your people need to flee north and seek shelter at Fort Richmond.'

Even as I said it, this sounded a little thin. Why on earth would anybody take heed of me?

'Where you from, boy? What's your authority?' asked the man, and I found myself lost for an answer. The women and children wandered up and were peering closely at me.

I said, 'A lot of Comanches have

crossed over from the Indian Nations. They're in the territory now and have already killed people. You got to leave right now.'

'We don't care in this town for anybody telling us what we should do,' said the man, 'nor are we keen on seeing guns.'

I couldn't make out at all what accent this man had. At first I thought English, but then I wasn't sure. He turned to the women and said, 'Sister, might I beg you to fetch one of the elders?'

'With a good will,' she replied. Giving me a suspicious look the woman took the children's hands and set off down the street. It wasn't difficult to see that I had not made a specially brilliant impression so far, but I was somewhat at a loss to know what else I could have done.

The man was still looking at me with what I interpreted as disapproval. Once the woman had been dispatched to fetch an 'elder', whatever that might mean, he said to me, 'While we're awaiting on our sister's return, I'll trouble you to hand over that gun at your belt. We'll have no deadly weapons on our streets in this town.'

Now this put me in something of a quandary. I didn't want to be at outs with these people or they might not take my advice seriously. On the other hand, nor did I wish to be left defenceless, with Indians swarming across the border into this part of the territory. While I was pondering the question, the man carried on staring hard at me and then said,

'Well? You going to do as I bid?'

Before I could think of an answer, the woman who had been sent on an errand to find an elder returned without her children but with a tall, muscular old man of about sixty or sixty-five. His snow-white hair fell over his shoulders and he had a long beard to match. When he came up he said to the man who had demanded my gun of me, 'Brother Seth, what's this I see?

Guns are the Devil's work. You know that as well as I do and yet here is a young man, as bold as Lucifer, carrying such in public.'

Brother Seth, for that was evidently the name and title of the man who wanted my gun, clenched his jaw until the muscles stood out like ropes in his neck. He said sullenly, 'I already asked him for it.'

'Asked?' said the old man in amazement. 'Do you *ask* a wolf to give up its prey? Do you *ask* the man of blood to forsake his wickedness? You do not. It is not mealy-mouthed requests that are needed in the present case, but strong words.' He marched up to me where I was seated on my pony, and said in a booming voice, like he was delivering a sermon in a big church, 'Boy! Hand over that firearm.'

I gained the feeling that this fellow was in the habit of having people listen to him and then do as he said. This can have a bad effect upon some people, because they start to think that they are more important than is actually the case. I was right ticked off about the situation, because I had only come to their damned town to save their lives and now they were bossing me about. I was more than half-minded to spur on my pony and just dig up and leave that town.

It could be that the old man, this elder that they minded, saw the thought cross my face, because of a sudden he lunged forward and grabbed my reins. Then with the other hand he reached up and grasped my arm firmly. He may have been as old as Methuselah, or so he seemed to me at my young age, but by golly there was an uncommon amount of strength in his muscles. So unexpected was the movement that I found myself tumbling from my horse and falling into the dust. It was then but the work of a moment for him to bend down and snatch the pistol from my holster. He then proceeded to hand it to the man called Brother Seth.

To show, presumably, that there was

no hard feelings about dealing with me so roughly, the old man then helped me get to my feet. As he did so, his arm brushed against my chest and he withdrew it as though he had been scalded. He then gave me a look of detestation and horror, and said to the woman who was still standing there silently and observing all that was happening without comment, 'Sister, we are all of us deceived. This is a woman, masquerading as a man. This is a disgusting thing, abhorrent to God and man.'

Well, I could not somehow share his view; for my own self there seemed to me to be many things in this world that are a sight worse than an adventurous girl putting on her brother's pants; but there it was. To these folk, girls dressing as boys and, for all I know to the contrary, boys dressing like their sisters, was obviously something shocking.

What had begun as an honest and selfless action on my part to save these people had now been turned on its head, leaving me as some sort of bad lot. I wasn't altogether sure how this had occurred. The old man still had hold of my pony's bridle, so that I wasn't able just to vault into the saddle and escape, leaving them to the mercy of the Indians. Not only that, but my father's pistol was in the safe keeping of Brother Seth, who was now looking at me like I was something lower than a skunk. Who would have thought that swapping clothes about would have been so frowned upon?

I might explain here that the people who had settled thereabouts were very hot for the Lord and felt that they had a better handle on the Lord's intentions and desires than any of the big churches. They were what some call 'primitive Christians'. They shared everything and helped each other out in every way.

That was all well and good, but the down side was that their leaders were forever ferreting around in Leviticus or Deuteronomy for something that folk enjoyed doing that was really sinful. Girls wearing boys clothes and vice versa was one of those things that apparently the Deity was dead set against, although for why I could not tell you.

So far I had managed to annoy the three citizens I had so far met in New Jerusalem, both by carrying a gun and by dressing as a boy. I guess that this was not a good beginning when it came to persuading them to abandon their homes purely on my say-so. Even if I had been dressed respectably and had ridden into that town unarmed and as meek and girly as you please, I still think that I would have encountered trouble there.

I had not realized this until the old elder said to me in that loud, preaching kind of voice, 'Something needs to be looked into here. You come here waving a gun about, disguised as a boy. Then you tell us we have to leave our homes unguarded and go from this town. What would be the next event, some gang of your friends rides in and steals all our belongings? Is that how it was planned, hey?'

I hadn't thought about it, but hearing the case so neatly set out in that way, I suppose that he had a point. He didn't know me from Adam and here I was, urging him and his neighbours to leave town at once. It must have sounded a bit odd. But I knew that this wasn't at all the case and I also knew what he did not: that a large body of Comanches were at this very moment sweeping through Kansas and most likely leaving murder and mayhem in their wake.

I said, 'If you people don't want to take notice of what I say, then leave me be and let me ride on to Fort Richmond. They have to be warned, because the army don't yet know of this.'

'And somebody has entrusted you with this important information that is unknown to anybody else in the territory, is that what you'd have us believe?' asked the elder, the incredulity showing plainly in his face. 'Do you take us for perfect fools?'

I started to give a stumbling explanation of the circumstances which had led up to my being given the responsibility of warning the cavalry about the invasion, but long before I had reached the end of my tale it was easy to see that none of the three people standing there, staring at me, believed a single word of what I was saying. The elder said, 'Sister, you must take this young woman to your home for now. Your husband is there, is he not?'

'Yes sir, that he is.'

'Then tell him to set a guard upon this person and not to listen to any fantastical stories which she might weave. Do not let her speak to your children. I charge you to keep her under your eye until this evening. We will judge this difficult matter at the meeting then. Perhaps the Lord will show me the way of it before then.'

I didn't say so at the time, but even then, young as I was, I thought that the

Lord was pretty regular in passing on his counsel to this man and that he then directed the footsteps of the little community in the way of righteousness. He seemed to have the place sewn up tight, with his word probably being on a level with that of the Lord of Hosts when it came to deciding any course of action.

For now, there was little enough that I could do and although I knew how pressing the danger was, there would be no point in bolting. I was sure that they would raise a hue and cry for me and how far was I likely to get on foot? The woman who was escorting me to her home said, 'What are you called?'

'My name's Elizabeth, but folk generally call me Beth.'

'Elizabeth is a beautiful name. It means, oath to God, but I guess you already know that?' I didn't, but I just smiled politely.

When we entered her house I saw at once an unsmiling man who was reading to the two children I had earlier seen with the woman. As soon as we went in the woman went over and whispered something in her husband's ear, all the while looking across at me.

He nodded his head and then came over to me, saying, 'I'm charged with keeping you safe until tonight's prayer meeting. I can't set a watch upon you, so I'll have to put you somewhere. He led me to a pantry at the back of the kitchen, a large, walk-in closet, whose shelves were filled with jars and bottles.

His wife followed us and handed me a Bible, saying, 'Seek ye the Lord while yet ye may.' Then the man gave me a slight shove to encourage me to enter the pantry and, once I was within, he closed and bolted the door behind him.

6

The first thing I did when once I'd heard the footsteps recede, was to start looking for a way to escape. This did not look very promising though, because the only window was a tiny one set high up in the wall. Even if I did manage to get up to it by clambering up the shelves or something of the sort, it would be too small for me to get through. Quite apart from that, the shelves themselves were flimsy and supported only by wooden pegs driven into the wall. They would be most unlikely to support my weight.

I came closer to despairing at that point than ever I had so far on my journey. Perhaps it was because there was nothing I could actually do, other than sit on the floor and wait for somebody to fetch me. At least when I had been chased by the Indians and so on, I was able to sublimate my anxiety and fear into vigorous, physical action. There was nothing whatever to be done now, though.

I have no idea how long I was sitting on that pantry floor before I heard somebody approaching. The door opened and the woman, whose name I still did not know, said, 'We wouldn't have you starve. We're Christians. Come, set at the table with us for our meal.'

Her husband was standing behind her, presumably in order to be on hand, should I try to make a run for it.

Once we were seated at the table, me, the man and wife and their two little children, the husband said a long and elaborate grace, invoking the blessing of the Lord on his family, me as a guest and also upon the food on the table. Then we began eating. It was only freshly baked bread, butter and cheese, washed down with milk, but I found it most satisfying. After he finished with the prayer, the man said to me,

'My name is Benjamin. This here is my wife Susan and these girls are called Esther and Miriam.'

'My name is Elizabeth.'

'So, Elizabeth,' said Benjamin, 'What is the story behind this wild escapade of yours?' Although he was a sober and godly man, there was a hint of amusement in his voice. I don't think that he saw me as the scout for a gang of robbers, but more likely to be a runaway of some kind.

As we ate I explained about taking my brother's place in the Pony Express and then told him of the horrible scene at Smoky Mountain. He listened carefully, asking one or two penetrating questions to clarify matters which were obscure to him. I said nothing of shooting the road agents, for I felt that this might prejudice him against me. I gave full details, though, of Joshua's death.

As I described the bloody scene at Smoky Mountain and talked of being chased by Comanches, Susan and her children looked at me in amazement, captivated by my narrative. Benjamin watched me more closely, trying I think to gauge how reliable and honest I was. When I had finished he sat back in his chair and eyed me narrowly. Then he said, 'This is true what you've told us? You have not embellished or exaggerated any of it?'

I was stung at the imputation of dishonesty and said hotly, 'I have no need to exaggerate. The real thing was enough.'

Turning to his wife, he said, 'What did Elder Joseph say of this, wife?'

'Said as we would enquire more deeply at the meeting this even.'

'Strikes me that there's no time to lose,' said Benjamin, 'This child's given us a true bill, we could be at hazard this very second.' He got to his feet.

'Where are you going, husband?'

'To see Elder Joseph and consult with him.'

'He won't thank you for questioning his decisions,' said Susan. 'If he says evening meeting, then that's what he means. Like as not he's praying about it this minute.'

'I'd sooner know that word has been sent to the cavalry at Fort Richmond,' said Benjamin, 'Than I would that that old man is on his knees in prayer.'

After her husband had left the house — without, incidentally, returning me to the pantry under lock and key — Susan gave me a reproachful look, as though I had brought trouble and disgrace to their home.

She said, 'It does no good, raising up a rebellion 'gainst the elders. I've told Benjamin that afore.' She paused for a second, then added, as though in some sort of apologetic explanation, 'My husband wasn't always saved.'

I hardly knew how to respond to any of this and contented myself with smiling at the children. I offered to help wash up the wares, which offer was accepted. I fancy that Susan too had been persuaded while I was talking that I was not really about to trick them into leaving their house so that a gang of bandits could enter it and rob them at will. As we worked, she asked me about my mother and whether she wouldn't be dreadfully worried about me by now, having expected me back long since. I agreed that this was very likely to be true.

Benjamin was gone for the best part of an hour and I was hardly able to contain myself during that time, so anxious was I to be on my way again. I had more or less taken it as read that there would be no question of the citizens of New Jerusalem following me north to the army base, and I thought now that the best practical way that I could aid them would be by bringing the cavalry down here to protect the town. But without a horse, it was very far from clear to me how I would be able to undertake even that operation.

During the course of the hour or so that I was compelled to spend in the company of Susan and her daughters, I found that they were not such a starchy bunch as I had first assumed. I kind of got the idea that there was so much religious observance in public that they had all got into the way of letting it all carry on over into their domestic lives.

When at last the street door opened and the head of the house returned, I had hope that things had reached some sort of arrangement, because Benjamin was carrying in my hand the pistol which had earlier been confiscated from me.

'Benjamin Carter,' exclaimed his wife when she caught sight of the gun, 'What are you about that you should bring such a wicked article into our home? In front of the little 'uns too. I should think you'd be ashamed to do it, sir!'

'Well now, don't take on so. I'm only returning some property to this young lady. You wouldn't have her sent off through dangerous country alone and unarmed, would you, wife?'

Susan looked at me and for a moment I thought that I detected the ghost of a smile around the corners of her mouth. I think that she had decided that I wasn't such a bad one after all.

She said, 'Happen not. I hope that you haven't fell out with the elders over this?'

'Not overmuch. Elder Joseph can be a hasty man and we'll say no more on the subject. This child meant well by us and I'll take oath she's no liar. That being so, the less we delay her, the better. For us, as well as others.'

Having delivered himself of these sentiments, Benjamin handed me the pistol, which I tucked gratefully back into the holster. The two girls were gazing up at me nervously, so I bent down and said, 'It's been right nice visiting with you. I hope we might meet again.' Then I stood up and said, 'Does this mean that I can have my pony back as well?'

'Yes. I went to see him. I saw the letter pouches. I reckon you're the genuine article all right.'

Susan came up to me and unexpectedly enfolded me in an affectionate embrace, kissing me on the cheek as she did so.

'I will own that I didn't care for the look of you at first,' she announced bluntly. 'But I hope I ain't one never to allow when I've been mistook. You're all right, Elizabeth, I'm sure of it. Go with God.'

Together, me and Benjamin walked down the street to the barn where my pony was. As we strolled along, he said, 'You mustn't judge us harshly. Sometimes we're a mite mistrustful of strangers. But we ain't so very bad, when once you get to know us. Sorry for shutting you up in the pantry.'

'You won't get in to trouble for disputing with that elder, I hope?'

'Ah, we'll both live it down. I wasn't always numbered among the saved, you know. Maybe I'm a little too worldly in my ways for my own good sometimes.'

I didn't know what to make of all that, having little notion in those days of what being 'saved' might entail. I was so relieved to be allowed to continue on my way that I have to say that I didn't much care, either.

I was glad to see that nobody had untacked the pony and that he was ready to go at once.

I said to Benjamin, 'Thank you for believing me, sir, and sticking up for me too.'

'I can tell an honest person when I meet one, Elizabeth. Whether or no they are saved. Get along with you now.'

I mounted up and was about to offer more thanks, when Benjamin said, 'Enough talk. God speed!' Then he slapped the pony's flank and cried, 'Yah!' I shot off like an arrow from a bow, heading north once more towards Fort Richmond.

I didn't know, and for that matter still do not to this day, what to make of the town of New Jerusalem. Were they good-hearted and kind people who feared the Lord? Or were they rather a stiff-necked set of pious types who mistrusted strangers who didn't fit into their own views on how to conduct life? I have never been able to decide.

One thing which those who love horses might have noted is that I refer to my pony only as that, without using any given name. Well, there's a good reason for that: I never found out what his name was! All I knew about him was that he was a gelding. Changing horses every ten miles or so, twelve times in the course of a working day, there was no time to become acquainted with the beasts. It was a case of jump off one and then vault right onto the next. Nobody introduced us and gave us time to get to know each other. I called him 'Pony' and that was enough for the both of us.

Now that I was free and on the right track, I was feeling a whole heap better about every aspect of my personal situation. True, there was still the very present danger of attack by hostile Indians, but of course when you're young you tend only to concern yourself with immediate threats to your well-being. So it was that despite seeing a number of men who had been slaughtered by Redskins, including one right in front of me, I was still able somehow to thrust the fear of such an eventuality as my own death right to the back of my mind. Instead, I focused only upon enjoying a ride in the late afternoon through some beautiful country.

It may seem hard to believe, but I had never in my life been in Kansas before, despite living right by the Missouri, which marked the boundary between the two territories. The land across which I was now making my way was similar in a geographical sense to Missouri, except that it was a lot wilder. It looked the way that it must have done around St Joseph, before all the farming began.

The road I was travelling along was no more than a dusty track, with hoofprints covering it, but few ruts from wheels, such as a wagon or stage might leave. It looked to me as though hardly anybody ever came along this way. The land undulated gently, with each rise revealing plains stretching into the distance.

It was after coming to the top of one such gentle hill that I caught my first glimpse of Fort Richmond. It was still some miles away and because of the haze looked to me as though it was floating above the ground. I had no scale with which to compare it, it must have been quite three or four miles off, but I could see, even at that distance, that it was very large. In addition to the great rectangular bulk of the fort itself, there were many other little shapes dotted around near it, some brown and others white. I couldn't for the life of me make out at all what these might be.

It was only as I came within a mile or so of Fort Richmond that I realized just how big it really was. The walls of the stockade must have been fifty feet high, and towering twice as high above them was a flagstaff from which was flying the stars and bars. Perched, as it seemed to me, precariously on the walls of the stockade were four structures, each the size of the average house. These were guard posts.

Now that I was nearer I could see that the objects which had so puzzled me were no more than tents. Some of these were bleached white army tents; others were the hide shelters of the Indians which they call tepees. After all that I had seen so far, I was more than a little taken aback to find a large number of Indians camped right around the fort. I wondered that the army tolerated it.

Later on I found that these people were not Comanches but another, peaceful tribe. They had pitched up close to the fort partly because this afforded them some protection from their more warlike neighbours, but also as the close proximity to so many soldiers gave them many opportunities to barter and trade with the men stationed at Fort Richmond.

I rode through what amounted to an Indian village before I reached the gates to the fort. To one side of the fort was an encampment of army tents, with chuck wagons parked near to them. It looked to me as though there were many more soldiers at the fort than was usual for them and this was some kind of overspill.

The gates stood wide open and although there was a cavalryman lounging about in front of them, there was no atmosphere of readiness. Inside the stockade, which was formed of roughly dressed tree-trunks erected vertically, side by side, I could see Indians talking to soldiers, and men in shirtsleeves milling about aimlessly. The sentry, if that is what he was, said casually, 'Anybody in especial you're hoping to see?'

'I need to speak to whoever's in charge.'

'You'll be lucky. What you sellin'?'

'Nothing at all. I have news for him.'

'Yeah, yeah. Sure you do. Tell me and I'll pass it on to him.'

I began to get agitated because, after all that I had been through, this stupid man was determined to hold me up even further. There is no telling what intemperate words I might have been driven to if an officer hadn't appeared on the scene at that moment.

He said to the sentry, 'What's going on, Rawlings? Who's this?'

I cut in at that point, saying, 'I'm a rider for the Pony Express. You might have heard of them.'

The officer looked at me sharply and said, 'Then what? What are you doing here?'

I gave him a brief account of the massacre at Smoky Mountain and he and the sentry both stared at me, hanging on what I said as though they hardly knew what to make of it all. When I had finished, he said to the soldier I had first spoken to, 'Rawlings, fetch the adjutant. At the double now. I'll stay here with this young fellow.'

After the sentry had set off at a brisk trot the officer said to me, 'You can dismount. By the look of your pony, you've ridden hard.'

I climbed down and the man looked closely at me. He didn't say anything, but I suspected that he might be entertaining some doubts about my sex. If so, he was too much of a gentleman to say anything, so I relieved him of the painful necessity by saying, 'I'm a girl, sir. It's a long story.'

'Yes, I dare say. Well, it's nothing to the purpose for now. This is a damned odd business.' Then, recollecting himself, he said, 'I beg your pardon, miss, it just slipped out.'

'I've heard worse. It's nothing.'

'Mind if I enquire as to your age?'

'I'm fifteen years of age.'

'God almighty!' he exclaimed and then hastily added, 'I'm sorry. But I never heard the like. Tell me, do you make a habit of exploits such as this?'

I wasn't sure how to frame a reply to this question, but fortunately Rawlings came back with a man who was saluted by the officer to whom I had been talking. These two went off out of earshot and had a brief consultation.

The upshot was that the adjutant, who introduced himself as Major Conway, asked if I would be kind enough to accompany him to the commanding officer's quarters. He spoke in a courteous and educated voice and treated me with such politeness that I almost felt like a grown-up person. This was something of a novelty after the way that I had been dealt with by various people up to that time.

As we walked across the square towards some buildings which were against the rear wall of the fort, Major Conway said, 'Just tell the officer all that you have told Captain Daniels. Stick to the facts, Miss . . . ?'

'Taylor. Beth Taylor. But please don't call me Miss Taylor, for it makes me feel like somebody's maiden aunt.'

He laughed at this and said solemnly,

'Very well. Beth it shall be.'

The officer in charge of the whole, entire fort was called Colonel Parker and he listened very closely to everything which I said, not interrupting at all until I had completed my account. Then he asked three or four questions, chiefly I think to make sure that I had left out no vital information. After that he sat back at his desk and drummed on the table-top with his fingers. I was sitting opposite him, but Major Conway was standing respectfully, if not to attention, then certainly not slouching.

'What do you make of all this, Conway?' asked the colonel.

'I believe it's a true bill, sir.'

'Yes, yes,' said Colonel Parker irritably, 'I make no doubt of that. I trust the girl perfectly. But how many men would you say that we might be facing?'

'It's hard to say, sir. There were better than a hundred at Crooked Creek. If that wasn't the main body, then I don't rightly know. Five hundred? Could be more.'

'And they could be anywhere in the territory. It's the hell of a thing. All right, sound muster. Let's get onto a war footing while we plan our next move.'

I think that Colonel Parker had almost forgotten about me while considering his military options, for he suddenly said, 'Miss Taylor, I suppose that you will be needing a bed for the night? I can't tell you how grateful we are to you for this. When things have settled down somewhat, I hope that we shall be able to talk at more length.'

This was all very pleasant and just exactly how I had hoped my news would be received. The adjutant offered to sort out somewhere for me to stay for the night and before going off to organize the men for action, he handed me over to a practical-looking half-breed woman, who, he said, looked after the spare rooms.

I said, 'My pony needs to be turned out. Will it be all right to put him in the corral I saw?'

'Yes, of course.'

'What about his tack?'

'There's a big tent for that. Just tell them that Major Conway said it was all right.'

It was coming on towards evening now and I was pretty well spent. There was a tiny little room which was used for guests and this was allocated to me. The woman said that she would have food sent to me and that she hoped that I would be comfortable there. Having said all this, she lingered and I thought it likely that people staying as the colonel's guests might be in the habit of tipping her. I had no money and so she was out of luck.

Now that I was left alone I kicked off my boots and lay down on the bed. After all that had happened, I was sure that I had now reached the end of my adventures, for what more could possibly befall me, surrounded by soldiers and in a fort belonging to the US Cavalry?

Which is just a small example of how

wrong one can be when trying to gauge
what the future might hold!

7

After what I had been through in the
last few hours it was hardly surprising
that almost as soon as I lay down on
that bed I promptly fell asleep. When I
awoke it was to find the room in
darkness. I had earlier noticed a lamp
standing on a little table, but I had not
the wherewithal to light it. In the
moonlight streaming through the
window, I saw that somebody had left
me a tray of food and a jug of water.
It was half a chicken, along with a
hunk of bread. I fell to and devoured
it ravenously.

I had no idea what time it might be,
but I could hear a lot of noise from
people talking and laughing, so I
figured that it couldn't be that late: not
the middle of the night or anything.
Nobody had said that I had to stay in
my room and since I had never before

been on an army base and perhaps would not get another opportunity to do so, I decided to go and explore a little.

One of the first things I noticed when I left the building in which I was staying and went into the main square of the fort, was that the mighty gates were still standing wide open. A single soldier was standing around at the gates, chatting to a couple of women, but other than that, anybody could come in and out. Young and inexperienced as I was, I felt instinctively that this was not a good way to carry on when there was a danger of attack.

As I wandered aimlessly across the square I was hailed by name, which greatly surprised me. Somebody called, 'Hey, Miss Taylor!'

I turned and saw the man called Rawlings, the soldier I had first met when I arrived at Fort Richmond. When he came nigh to me, he said, 'You're the theme of general conversation, you know. Never knew one girl to stir up so many people.'

'I don't rightly understand you,' I replied. 'Who've I stirred up?'

'Why, only the whole fort. Everybody's left, you know.'

I was still feeling a little muzzy and sleep-befuddled. I said, 'I'm sorry, I've been sleeping. Who has left?'

'Why,' said Rawlings, 'All those men as were encamped outside here and 'most every person from this fort. There's hardly but twenty of us been left behind. Everyone else has gone off to hunt for the Comanches you told 'em of. Say, tell me the truth, Miss Taylor. Did you send 'em off on a snipe hunt for the hell of it?'

So merry and free with his speech was the man that I looked a little harder at him. It was not my eyes, though, that provided confirmation of what I had suddenly suspected: it was my nose. As Rawlings swayed nearer to me I caught the unmistakable odour of whiskey on his breath. The man was inebriated!

'I don't know anything about all this,'

I told him a little coldly. 'I just explained what I knew to your colonel. Whatever action he's taken after that is nothing to do with me.'

'Well, it's surely given us a little holiday!' said the intoxicated soldier cheerfully. 'So whether or no, I'm greatly obliged to you.'

I turned away in some disgust, but then, as I walked away, I said, 'Who's in charge of this fort now? Is the colonel still here?'

'Not he! Catch him missing out on a moment of glory. He rode out at the head of the column an hour back.'

'So who is looking after this place?'

'Senior officer is Lieutenant Bryson. But he's in the sack with some young lady. I tell you straight, tonight we're standing easy.'

I felt uneasy after talking to Rawlings, because from all that I could apprehend, Fort Richmond was now in the hands of a lot of foolish young men, some of who had no more sense than grasshoppers. I thought that I would go and check up on my pony. Although he was not mine, I felt a responsibility for the mount which had been provided for me by the Pony Express and wished to ensure that I would be returning him to his rightful owners in prime condition.

Once through the gates and out of the fort I could see many small fires burning outside the tepees. There were so many of these that I wondered momentarily whether the Indians hereabouts did not now outnumber the cavalry. I felt a little concerned notwithstanding the fact that I had been assured of the friendliness of this particular tribe. The plain before the fort was a twinkling constellation of little fires.

It was sheer chance that when everything began I was out in the corral and not sleeping in the room which had been assigned to me. The corral was set up in the lee of Fort Richmond's mighty wooden walls. It contained only a half-dozen other animals, in addition to my own. The pony seemed to be in good company and I was about to leave the corral when something extraordinary occurred. From the top of the wall, some fifty feet about my head, a body fell and came crashing to the ground. I looked up, but could see nobody there and guessed that whoever had just plummeted down must have toppled from the walkway which ran around the top of the wall.

As I jumped over the fence of the corral and ran to where the figure lay, silent and still, I was thinking that there must have been some kind of tragic accident: a man fainting perhaps, or tripping over the edge by clumsiness. I recall wondering, though, even as I approached the prone body, why there had been no cry of alarm as the man fell down.

When I reached the man I could see at once that he was not stirring at all and nor could I hear breathing. I did something which my brother had once taught me, which was to feel on the throat for a pulse. Not that I really expected this person to be dead, it was just that I had never had occasion to use this method in a real-life situation. So I crouched down and began fumbling around the side of his neck, where it was possible to feel for a pulse.

To my disgust I found that my hand was slippery with some liquid and I thought that maybe it was dribble. I jerked away and saw that the hand which had touched the throat looked black in the moonlight, as if I had grasped a handful of tar or something.

Then, of a sudden, the explanation hit me. The dark substance was blood and the reason why this man had not cried out as he fell was that he was already dead or dying when he was pitched over the top of that wall. From the quantity of blood I hazarded a guess that his throat had been cut.

While I was digesting the strange implications of my discovery, and before I had had a chance to become at all disturbed, I heard a shriek of fear, a woman's voice, which was abruptly cut off. It was not difficult to work out that the fort might be under attack by enemies and that it was defended only by a skeleton crew of drunken libertines.

★   ★   ★

Once the woman's screaming had been briefly heard, things moved very rapidly. As I got to my feet, the first shot came: from a rifle by the sound of it. Then there was shouting, which sounded as though it might be soldiers in the fort raising the alarm. This was followed by one or two more shots and then a perfect fusillade of rifle fire.

Now I might have been little more than a child at that time, but even so I figured that there was no percentage in being anywhere near a bunch of angry or fearful men firing off rifles in the dark. You just know that this is apt to end badly. So it was that I moved closer to the wall of the fort, in order to melt into the shadows until I knew properly what was going on.

This did not take long to figure and it tied in very well with the apprehensions that I had had about the gates of Fort Richmond standing wide open while the few soldiers within became intoxicated or otherwise fooled around like they might have been in a sporting house.

As I watched I could see men running from the tepees and racing towards the gate of the fort. Again, it didn't need a master of military strategy to work out what had chanced. Some of the Comanches had infiltrated the peaceful village camped outside Fort Richmond and had now entered the place and taken full advantage of the lack of preparation which existed now that the commanding officer and other senior officers had departed.

I guessed that other Comanche warriors had probably been waiting near by until nightfall and now saw their opportunity to kill and loot at will. Then again, young as I was, I knew that if you were a girl there were things other than killing or looting to worry about. I had only the vaguest idea on the subject, but knew that I had best not show myself while these fellows were on the rampage.

So it was that I was the only white witness to the sacking and burning of Fort Richmond, which was one of those events that later came to define the year before the Civil War broke out.

After that first flurry of screaming, shouting and shooting, the only thing I heard was men speaking in a language that was not English. Then there came the sound of smashing glass and many heavy thuds. From where I was huddling, right against the exterior wall of the fort, it was clear that all these noises were coming from the central square, which you came upon as soon as you passed through the gates. That there was no more shooting or scream-ing was ominous, suggesting as it did that any resistance had been pretty well quashed early on in the attacks.

I knew that I should be making tracks out of that area, but the problem was to find the best way of slipping inconspicuously away while several hundred Indians went crazy with the desire for blood and fire. Because now that those in the fort had either been killed or otherwise silenced, the Comanches set out to to destroy the place entirely. The roughly dressed tree trunks that made up the walls of Fort Richmond were fixed side by side, but not precisely so; there were many cracks and gaps between one trunk and another. Through these I could see flickering lights and dancing shadows which told of more than one fire having been kindled within the fort.

My position was now becoming increasingly desperate. The horses in the corral, including my own pony, were growing restless as they smelled the smoke and perhaps caught glimpses of the flames. Some primeval fear was upon them and if I didn't get my pony away from this scene soon, he might

139

become ungovernable with fear.

Moreover I needed his tack, which was in a large tent nearby that served the purposes of a tack room or barn. One comforting circumstance was that I had not yet caught sight of any mounted men. From what I was able to see, all the Indians were on foot; if once I could get that pony cantering away with me on his back, then we might be safe, at least for a spell.

Just as I was screwing up my courage to the sticking point, as some old poet put the case, I realized that a tall man was striding in my direction with a flaming torch in his hand. At first I was naturally a-feared that he had seen me and was minded to put an end to my life, but this was not how things stood. Rather than being intent on causing mischief or harm to me, this wretch was about to set fire to the tent in which my saddle and bridle were currently stowed. Indeed, with no ado, he thrust the brand against the fabric of the tent and held it there until the canvas had begun to blaze. Then he simply turned on his heel and went back in the direction from which he had come.

Before going on, I have to admit that I was mightily puzzled by this behaviour at that time. You might have thought that the Indians would want the saddles and other material in the tent so that they could take the spare horses for their own. There were two explanations for this. The first was that these boys had taken some kind of oath that they would offer up the goods belonging to the army as some burnt offering to their gods. The other reason for this crazy conduct was that somehow they had found a crate of whiskey and were busily engaged in drinking themselves stupid. Both of which made for a pretty lethal combination.

Unless I acted quickly there would be no possibility of escape on horseback, so I gritted my teeth and ran to the burning tent. The flap sealing the entrance was closed with buckled straps and I did not have the time or inclination to fiddle about opening it. Fortunately, by this time a large hole in one wall of the tent had been eaten away by the fire, and I thought that I might be able to risk jumping through it, so gaining access to the tent. Jumping into a burning structure in that way is not something most of us will be able to do without a lot of hesitation, but what spurred me on was a dull boom from near by, which sounded like a barrel of powder going up. The horses were now neighing and whinnying, and if I left it any longer they would most likely be kicking down the fences and vanishing into the night. I took a brief run and then leaped through the hole and into the tent.

There was more smoke in the tent than I had bargained for, and at least a dozen saddles. Luckily, mine was distinctive enough, with the *mochila* and all. Finding the bridle took a little longer and by then I was coughing and choking with all the smoke that I had inhaled.

The night was rent with warbling war cries as the flames took hold of Fort Richmond. There were sparks floating up into the sky now, and it surely would not be long before those stout and all but impregnable walls themselves went up in smoke. Now that I was near my pony, talking calmly and fastening on his saddle, he calmed a little, but he was not at all happy about the strange noises, sights and smells. His natural instinct was probably to bolt and there was a limit to how long I would be able to restrain this impulse. I just hoped that I would be securely on his back when he did make a break for it.

The gate to the corral was padlocked and it was necessary for me to heave a few parts of the fence down to make a way for the animals to run free. By the time I had finished that, flames were licking the top of the walls of Fort Richmond and it was not hard to see that the structure would, by morning, be reduced to a charred ruin.

Not having the least notion of where to go for the greatest safety, I led the pony away from the the Indian tepees and in the general direction of the part of the plain that appeared to me to be least inhabited. Not wanting to attract attention by generating the noise of hoof beats, I waited until we were a quarter-mile from the fort before I mounted. Even then I maintained only a sedate trot for a time.

Before I risked speeding up a little I paused and turned back to survey the scene. The whole fort was alight now and the blaze must have been visible for miles. If anybody doubted that there was now a full-scale Indian rebellion in progress, then that massive bonfire alone would be enough to convince them of their error.

I did not feel inclined to travel through the whole night. The risk of laming my horse in the darkness apart, I had no idea at all what the morrow would bring and wished to be fresh and ready to tackle anything. On coming to a sizeable forest I dismounted and led the pony in among the trees. When once I was assured that, even in daylight, nobody would be able to see us from the open country that lay beyond the edge of the wood, I tethered the horse and lay down to sleep.

It says in Scripture: *Morning brings counsel,* which is merely another way of asserting that you feel better after a good night's sleep and more able to tackle the world. I knew now what I ought to be doing, although the precise details were not plain to me.

In my head, before I had fallen asleep, I had been maintaining a running tally of distances and I calculated that I had travelled about a hundred and fifty miles west of the Missouri river and then ridden fifty miles north. Surely, if I now headed south-east, I could not fail to strike the trail that I had been on, on the outward journey?

If so, I could find a Pony Express

station, hand over the mail and then take the next pony eastbound. The more I turned this project over in my mind, the sounder it appeared to be. The greatest advantage was that it would get me clear of this Comanche war now raging hereabouts. This then was one of the tentative plans I was mulling over, shortly before I drifted off.

The sun was streaming through the leaves overhead and it promised to be a fine day. Perhaps you have at one time opened your eyes in the morning with the feeling that something has woken you up, rather than your just having come to naturally? That was just how it was when *I* opened my eyes and saw the bright light trying to fight its way through the fresh young leaves which were bursting from their buds on the branches overhead. I lay for a second or two, trying to bring to mind whether I might perhaps have dreamed something, which might have been what awakened me. Then there came the sound of a dry twig snapping underfoot and at once I knew that there was somebody — a person — who was moving about, very stealthily, near by.

It's a strange thing, and I have noticed this often over the years, that a human person treading on something in a wood makes an altogether different sound from an animal like a deer or dog. I couldn't explain this in words, but maybe readers will know what I am talking about. Anyways, I was aware that somebody was moving about near me: somebody who didn't want to be heard.

I reached down for my pistol, which I had propped up beside my boots when I took them off. I cocked it and then called out, as deep as I could manage,

'Who's there? If you don't want a ball through your head, you best step forward, right sharpish.'

My words worked to some effect, because there was a crackling of undergrowth and, to my amazement, the trooper who had been on sentry duty when I first fetched up at Fort Richmond came into view.

'Lord a mercy!' I exclaimed. 'Mr Rawlings. What in tarnation are you doing here?'

'I walked here last night,' he said with a sheepish air, that I found puzzling, 'only got here an hour since, if that.'

'What happened at the fort? How did you escape?'

Rawlings looked evasive; one might almost have said shifty. He said, 'I managed to outwit those Indians. Here I am.'

Then it struck me: what had befallen all this man's comrades in arms? There had been women at that fort, what you might call camp followers. Had any of the soldiers done their duty and protected these helpless folk?

I said, 'What became of everybody else, Mr Rawlings?'

'Like I told you, I walked here — '

'Walked?' I said contemptuously. 'You mean you *ran*. Did you leave all those poor people, the women and so on, to their fate? What of your friends? Did you fight with them side by side?'

The solider grew red in the face and said angrily, 'Don't you speak so to me. What's it to do with you, anyway?'

The thought of this coward running away from danger and leaving everybody else to die filled me with loathing.

I said, 'It's nothing to me. Not a thing. You make your way and I'll make mine. I have to get moving now.'

It was the first time that I had really looked at this young man and I realized that he really was very young indeed. I couldn't think that he was more than two or three years older than me. When I said that about leaving, he looked crestfallen and for a second I almost thought that he was going to burst into tears.

Then he said, 'I don't know what to do.'

'How so? You saved your skin. Seems to me as you have a talent for getting by.'

'You don't understand. I left my post.'

'Yes, I should just about say that you did that all right.'

'But you ain't supposed to, not in the army. It's what they call desertion.'

'I guess then as they'll be angry about it. It's nothing to me.'

Rawlings looked positively desperate. He said, 'You still don't get it. Desertin' in the face of the enemy, that's what they call a capital crime. I heard it said as you can be shot for it. I'm scared of dying, Miss Taylor, and that's the God's honest truth.'

8

I had thought a few seconds earlier that Rawlings looked mighty upset about things, but now his eyes really were bright with what looked to me awful much like unshed tears. I affected not to notice and began putting on my boots. As I did so, I asked, 'You got a gun with you, at least?'

'No, I left my rifle behind.'

'A pistol?'

'No, I ain't got anything at all, no how.'

This was exasperating, for I had hoped that the two of us would make a stronger combination than either of us by our own selves. As it was, I couldn't in anywise see how teaming up with this callow boy would be to my advantage.

I said, 'What happened? You throw your weapons away when you ran?'

The young trooper didn't answer directly, but said, 'Two months back, just after I enlisted, we was given a talk on army law, what you call military law, you know. The officer, he told us most forceful that the worstest thing any soldier in the US Army can be guilty of is casting away his arms in the face of the enemy. Said as any one of us as did that, we'd be like to get ourselves shot for it. I'm a-feared that that there is just what I done.'

'Sounds likely enough,' I replied, 'but it's still no affair of mine.'

Despite my hard words to this boy, I knew in my heart of hearts that I could not just abandon him here. I had been hoping that somebody would come and take care of *me*, and now I was put into a position where I was to assume responsibility for somebody else's welfare.

This was not at all what I had planned for and although I was going to try and save him as well, I made up for it by being as cruel in words as I knew how. My only excuse is that I was well vexed about the whole business. Then another thought came to me and I said,

'You on foot? You didn't think to bring with you a horse or even a donkey?'

'Nothing o' the sort. I come here just on my own two feet.'

This put yet another complexion on things, because instead of cantering along at a smart lick and being able to outpace anybody on foot who was being hostile, travelling along of a boy walking would slow me down no end. I was, by my own free decision, bound to another person whose presence was at best an embarrassment and could, at worst, put me in hazard of my life.

In later years, I came to see this as the time when I truly grew up, having been before that time pretty careless of others and not minded to alter my plans for the convenience of anybody in the world, other than my mother and brother. That day, though, I took on the role of protector for a stranger who meant less than nothing to me. It was my first act of adult life and marked, as I see it now in retrospect, my childhood's end.

I felt obscurely that I had been buffaloed into assenting to a proposition which was little enough to my liking and, since there was nobody else to take it out on, I was gruff and ungracious with the object of my charity.

Once I had my boots on and had strapped on my pistol, I said, 'Well, I guess I can't prevent you from walking along of me, but for the Lord's sake, pull yourself together and act like a man. I had it in mind to head south-east. You have any better plan?'

At being spoken to almost civilly in this way and having his opinion solicited, the soldier became anxious to please, like a puppy who has in the past been kicked and is now being petted and stroked.

He said, 'Golly, Miss Taylor, I don't know the country hereabouts in the least degree. I only was posted up here less than a fortnight since. After what they call basic training, you know.' In a burst of confidence, he added, 'Tell you the truth, this here is my first posting.'

It was on the tip of my tongue to tell Rawlings that unless I missed my guess, his posting at Fort Richmond was likely to be his last, and that he would most probably end up in some military jail for his escapade of the night before, but I held my own counsel, saying instead, 'If we're going to spend any time together, then we can't go round calling each other *Mister* Rawlings and *Miss* Taylor. My name's Beth. What do they call you?'

'My name's Tom.'

'Well then, Tom, we best get moving. I reckon you won't have any food with you?'

'Not a morsel.'

'Then we'll have to do without breakfast.'

It was a fine day for hacking out, but of course I was limited to a walk, on account of I had this young fellow trudging along at my side. I wondered if I ought to take turns on the pony and offer him the chance to rest his feet, but the more I considered the idea, the more absurd it seemed. He was, after all, a professional soldier, while I was little more than a schoolgirl. If he wanted a horse, then he would have to acquire one for his own self. Besides which, my own mount did not belong to me and I had no authority to go lending it out to any passing stranger.

In those first couple of hours, I learned a great deal about Tom Rawlings: from his age, which was eighteen, to the farm where he grew up, which was in Missouri. He was a regular chatterbox and before long I had pretty well tired of his company. From my point of view the most annoying part of the situation in which I found myself was that I was forced to travel real slow, keeping pace with a fool who appeared to have little to say that was worth hearing.

Soon after we set out I found that we were crossing what looked to be some kind of track. It was heading east, rather than south, but I thought it might lead us somewhere. My belly was starting to make noises of discontent and a bite to eat surely would not come amiss.

I said, 'You got any money for food, should we some across a body who's willing to sell us such?'

'Got ten dollars. Think that'll meet the case?'

'I reckon so. Even a farmhouse might part with some bread, maybe cheese as well.'

In the event we did better than a mere farmhouse, because after following the track for six or seven miles we stumbled upon an entire town.

Sometimes you come to towns which are vibrant and bursting with life. There are buildings going up on vacant lots, with all the attendant sounds of hammering and sawing; coaches and carts rumble along the street, telegraph wires hum overhead and all the other signs are there to indicate that here is somewhere which is growing, rather than shrinking.

Some towns though, give out quite the opposite impression. They come across as sluggish and tired, with little happening on their streets. Sometimes they almost have the air of a ghost town about them, with not a soul to be seen. So it was with the little burg upon which we chanced late that morning and which rejoiced in the optimistic name of Eldorado, although we only found that out later.

I will say a few words about what I later heard of this town, to make things a little clearer. Some good few years before we fetched up in the vicinity, somebody had made a strike of silver in the nearby hills. There had been a rich vein of the precious metal mixed in with lead ore. There was a rush of prospectors, all of whom thought that they might be going to make their fortunes. It was not uncommon in the decades before the War between the

States for little towns to spring up overnight in this way, like mushrooms.

Some of them flourished and grew into sizeable cities, while others faded into obscurity in a matter of months, as soon as the silver or gold upon which their prosperity depended ran out. Others though, hung on tenaciously and refused to die, even though there was nothing really keeping the inhabitants there any more or tying them to that particular spot. This is how it was with Eldorado.

There had been at its peak almost a thousand people living in and camped around the town. As the silver became harder to extract and the lead ore diminished in quality, so that it was barely worth smelting, most of these people drifted off to try their luck elsewhere.

There remained in the town a core of maybe three or four dozen people, men chiefly, with only a tiny handful of women and even fewer children. They might not have been making a fortune there, but they were independent and free, with no interference from any official body. They grubbed out just about enough silver to keep body and soul together and were happy to stay put.

Like I say, I didn't learn all this until a good while later and then only because of the tragic events in the town during the Civil War. But I digress.

As we came nigh to the little huddle of wooden buildings, there was no sign at all of life. Somewhere a door or something was creaking mournfully as it swung back and forth in the breeze, but, other than that, the place was as silent as a tomb.

'I don't like it,' said Tom Rawlings. 'Something's amiss. You think the folk here been killed by Indians?'

'I wouldn't have said so. There's no bodies as I can see, and, from what I know, they burn and loot wherever they go.'

Although I had very little more than he did in the way of experience of the

Comanches, Rawlings listened to me carefully, as though I were some kind of expert on the subject; which was highly gratifying.

While we were hanging round there, on the edge of this town, surveying its run-down and dingy appearance, a man came out of one of the nearby buildings and said sharply, when once he caught sight of us,

'What are you two staring at? You think my house is an exhibition in a museum or some such?'

'I'm sorry,' I said. 'We didn't think that anybody lived here.'

Upon hearing this the man, who was perhaps in late middle age, laughed a little ruefully and said,

'You may well observe so, miss. You may well think that. There ain't a whole heap o' folk livin' here now and that's a fact. Was you hoping to meet somebody in especial?'

'We were looking to get some vittles. We can pay. Been riding since dawn and haven't yet ate.'

The man looked us over and decided that we were unlikely to be bandits or marauders. He said,

'There's no store here any more, nor anything like. But if you just wish to break your fast upon bread and a slice or two of meat, I reckon as I can accommodate you.' He added, 'There's no call for cash to change hands. You can pay me by telling me any news you picked up. We're a little behind with the world out here.'

Since I was ravenously hungry and the offer seemed well meant, I readily assented, and so me and Tom Rawlings went with the man into his home. It was sparsely furnished, although comfortable and clean.

'My name's Clinton,' he announced, 'What do they call you two?'

We gave him our names and he remarked, casually enough, 'I ain't so much up in the ways of ordinary life, not since I moved here ten years ago, but a girl travelling with a young horse soldier without a horse, well, I'll warrant that's still a rare enough sight. What's the case? You deserting your unit and running off with this young maiden?'

So eager was young Tom to rebut this calumny that he almost choked in his desire to explain that he was in fact not a deserter at all. His initial protestation sounded pretty thin to my ears and so I assisted him by setting out a story which I had been dreaming up over the course of the morning, with a view to saving the young soldier's neck.

Before Rawlings could come out with whatever nonsensical story he was hoping would excuse his desertion, I said, 'The truth is, sir, Mr Rawlings here rescued me at considerable risk to his own life.'

'Why, you don't say so? Tell me what happened.'

'I was staying at Fort Richmond. You might have heard of it, it's not so very far from here. The Comanches attacked and burned the place to the ground. This soldier, though, he hazarded his life to bring me to safety and I am eternally grateful to him for doing so.'

The man called Clinton cast his eyes from one to the other of us and then said, 'It's a remarkable story.' There was an ambiguity in the way that he stressed slightly the word *story* and I thought to myself, there's a man who knows a pail of eyewash when somebody tries to sell him it! He said nothing more though, and went to find the food which he had promised us.

As we ate Clinton said, 'What's all this about Comanches?'

Tom Rawlings began to say something, but the man interrupted him and said, 'Let your friend tell me about it, son. I've a suspicion that she knows somewhat more of this than you.'

'I'm a rider for the Pony Express — ' I began.

'The what?'

I was obliged to give him a brief account of the formation of the Pony Express and also of my adventures: those as touched on the burning of the

Smoky Mountain station.

Clinton said, 'This here Pony Express, they take on girls as well as boys?' I shrugged and he continued, 'There's a heap o' stuff you left out, but that's your business, I reckon. Tell me, the Comanches are on the rampage hereabouts, is that the crux of it?'

'That's pretty much it, yes.'

'I needs must tell others of this. You youngsters'll be fine by your selves for a spell?'

I assured him that we were only too happy to rest and eat and drink, so he left at once. After he had gone Rawlings said, 'Why'd you shame me so?'

'What in the Sam Hill are you talking about?'

'He was talking to you like you know it all and I don't know nothing. It ain't right. When all's said and done, I'm a soldier and you just a girl.'

I took a deep breath before answering this amazing attack. Then I said, 'If it escaped your notice, I just told a heap

165

of lies there to save you from getting hung or shot by the army. I'd think you'd be grateful to me for that.'

He had the decency to look a little shamefaced when I said that and remarked only, 'I'm tired of folk treating me like a kid.'

'Then start acting like a grown-up man,' I replied tartly.

The two of us sat there in a moody and ill-tempered silence for the next quarter-hour, neither feeling inclined to make the peace. It was therefore something of a relief when Clinton came back with three tough-looking men, all about the same age as him, which is to say fifty or so. These men eyed me and Rawlings dubiously and generally gave the overall impression that they were the sort who were adept at detecting imposture and deceit in others.

My heart sank, because I did not think that my little fairy tale about how Rawlings had rescued me would pass muster under close questioning but, as it turned out, they asked nothing about this at all. Instead, one of the men said, 'What's this about Comanches? How many and where did you see them?'

This was easier, because I was able to give a brief description of the events at Smoky Mountain, tell them what the guide there had said and also set out what the colonel at Fort Richmond had said and done, following with an eyewitness account of the destruction of the fort.

When I had finished, one of the men turned to the others and said shortly, 'That sounds like a true bill.' The others nodded. One of them looked very hard at me and said, 'You a boy or a girl?'

'I'm a girl.'

'Well, what are you doing tricked out like that?'

'I've been riding hard. Come nigh on two hundred miles in the last couple o' days.'

The man considered this for a moment and then said, 'I wish my girl had half your grit.' I didn't at all know how to respond to that and so remained silent.

'We need to make provision, less'n we're attacked,' said the third of the men, who had not yet spoken. Turning slightly to me, he asked, 'You can shoot?'

'I can shoot,' I told him.

He looked then at Tom Rawlings and said, 'What about you, son? You got a weapon?'

'No, sir.'

'Happen we can settle that. You fire a rifle?'

'I'm a soldier.'

'Huh,' said the man, 'that don't signify. Still, one more gun with us is all to the good.'

These men all struck me as somewhat taciturn and grim but, at the same time, men you might be glad to have on your side if things got tough. They treated me well enough, affording me the respect due to a youngster who has, as they say, won his spurs.

The young soldier though, was the

object of curious side glances. I don't know whether Clinton had told them the story I concocted, but I have a suspicion that for some reason they didn't think much to Rawlings. Maybe they were eyeing him askance because he had neither horse nor gun and gave every sign of having left his post speedily. Whatever the reason, they didn't appear to take to him as they did to me. Rawlings, I think, was aware of this and piqued by it.

The four men, including Clinton whose house we were in, left. I imagined that they would be alerting the other people living in the town to the threat that faced them.

As soon as they had gone, Rawlings said, 'There you go again, putting on side.'

I was getting heartily sick of hearing this foolishness by now and I told him, 'You want people to treat you better, you best start acting different. More like a grown up and less like a baby.'

He got to his feet and commenced to go red in the face. At first I thought he might be about to burst into tears, but instead he almost shouted, 'You are one stuck-up devil, you know that?' I pointedly ignored him and he then made the serious mistake of coming closer and saying in that same loud voice, 'You best mind me, I'm telling you or — '

This was just the kind of situation that I was skilled at handling, having had any number of such rows with my brother. As the young soldier advanced, still red in the face and angry at what he saw as being slighted both by me and others, I suddenly stretched out my leg and hooked his ankles, tugging sharply.

As I did this, I said, 'Or what?'

He toppled over. I jumped up and then dropped astride Rawlings's chest, pinning him down.

I said, 'We best get something clear right now, Tom Rawlings. You try and threaten me like that, you gonna come off worst for sure. You hear what I tell you?'

I have to say that I do not think that this young man had had much experience of wrestling. Had it been my brother, he would have managed to tip me off him without too much effort, but the boy on whose chest I was sitting seemed bewildered by the turn of events. He made a token struggle and then just lay there helplessly, staring up at me.

We stayed like that for a second or two, me thinking that I had in a satisfactory way demonstrated that I was his superior not only in the various ways which we had already seen, but also when it came to physical fighting. I was about to say something to that effect when Rawlings announced, to my unutterable surprise, 'I never been with a girl.'

I looked down at the boy whom I was straddling and said coldly, 'That is entirely more than I wish to know. Why are you telling me that?'

Then the man whose house this was poked his head round the door and surveyed the scene impassively.

He said, 'I don't know what you two are up to, but one of our fellows has been up on the side of the mountain. He says there's a whole bunch of riders heading this way. You going to help or fool about like children?'

I scrambled to my feet and gave Rawlings a venomous look. Then I said to Clinton, 'I'm ready for anything, sir.'

9

In the winding single street of the town were gathered perhaps thirty or forty men. All were carrying weapons of some description, mainly rifles and scatterguns. There were also four, maybe five women. These also had guns and looked to me as though they knew how to handle them as well. I wondered if this was the first time that this little place had been menaced by an attack of this kind.

Clinton came up to me and young Tom Rawlings and I saw that he was carrying a rifle under his arm and, in the other hand held a sawn-off scattergun.

He said to Tom, 'This is good for close-up work, but don't fire until your target is only twenty feet or so away.' He handed over the weapon and then turned to me, saying, 'You ever handle anything other than that pistol at your hip?'

'Shotgun a few times, but I never got the hang of it.'

'Best you stick to the pistol then. You want to stay here and help guard the little 'uns?'

'There's children here?' I asked in surprise.

'One or two. You want to go down the way and set with them and another woman, or will you come and lend your gun? We can do with every bit of help.'

My heart was pounding away like a steam hammer because this was the first time that I had really been given any choice in what I had been mixed up in since leaving home. In all the other incidents I hadn't really had time to weigh up the advantages and disadvantages. Now, if I took part in something, I would only have my own self to blame if things went wrong.

I said, 'I'm game to come along of you and the others.'

'That's right,' said Clinton. 'I thought

you would.' I wondered how old he thought I was or whether things were in such a desperate case that he wasn't really fussed about such a minor detail.

The riders had been spotted approaching from roughly the south, which suggested that these might be the same boys who had burned Fort Richmond to the ground. The way that the town of Eldorado was arranged was that it lay along the flank of a large hill with a craggy, almost cliff-like side. It was here that the mine workings had been established.

The town curved around the side of the hill and since the riders were heading straight towards us, this meant that any defenders attempting to prevent enemies getting close to the town would have to set up on the open land stretching away from the hill.

I said to Clinton, 'You don't think these might be the cavalry who left Fort Richmond last night, like I told you?'

'Thought on that. If so, then it'll do no harm to meet 'em halfway. I wouldn't have thought it, though. We'll see.'

I hadn't been looking forward to standing in the open grassland facing an oncoming rush of ruthless Comanche warriors, but it wasn't as bad as I had feared. At different times masses of rock had broken away from the hill: everything from great boulders to loose scree. I hadn't seen this, because we had come to the town from a different angle.

What it came to, then, was that we each selected a handy boulder or chunk of rock to shelter behind, so that we had the town at our back and the plain in front of us. When we started setting up there, I said to Clinton, 'I don't see any riders. You think they might have passed us by?'

'No, they were a right smart distance off when Lonny saw them. He could only make out the dust they was kicking up. No reason to think they're galloping. If they are coming on at a trot, they might not be here for another quarter-hour yet.'

Tom Rawlings went off to join a bunch of men some distance away, which was not an altogether displeasing circumstance. I had had about enough of his company to last me for a good long while and had no inclination to fight alongside him. I found myself crouching behind a large rock in the lee of which was a grim-faced woman of about forty. She said, 'What brings you here, honey?'

'It's a long story, ma'am . . . ' I began.

'I'll be bound,' she said. 'So happen it will keep until after we drive off those varmints.'

I saw that the woman had, resting on the rock behind which we were sheltering, an old-looking but no doubt serviceable musket. At her side was a flask of powder, a pile of balls and scraps of lint. The sight of these provisions reminded me that my own flask was in the saddlebag on the pony and that I had neglected to consider the fact that two of the chambers in my pistol were empty and I had not the wherewithal to do anything about it.

I said shyly, 'I don't suppose you could let me have a pinch of powder for my piece, could you, ma'am?'

At this, the stern visage of the woman split into a grin and she gave a wheezing chuckle.

'Lordy,' she said, all but overcome with mirth, 'If that don't beat all! You sit there and ask me for a pinch of powder, like you might be begging a little snuff. You're something else again, you know that, child? Here, help yourself to the makings.'

I thanked her and then proceeded to load the two chambers of my pistol which I had emptied at the bandits, what seemed like an age ago. The woman watched me without speaking until I had finished and then remarked, 'You surely handle that gun easily. I'm guessing that you've had much experience.'

'Only in firing at targets, in general,' I replied. Then, because this was the first conversation I had really had with a woman since it all happened, I added, 'Apart from two road agents I shot, that is.'

'You shot 'em? They die of it?'

'Yes ma'am, the both of them.'

The woman shook her head and repeated what she had said earlier: 'If that don't beat all!'

Our chatting was interrupted at this point by a man who was positioned as lookout on a nearby slope calling, 'They's a-comin'!'

I caught my breath and peeped nervously over the top of the boulder, to see that a group of riders, still the better part of a mile away from what I was able to judge, were now bearing down on our position. It was hard to gauge accurately in that brief glimpse, but I thought that there must have been upwards of fifty horses.

'You goin' to cock your piece or just sit there pantin' like a hog in a heat wave?' enquired the woman at my side. 'You want to have the hysterics, now ain't the best o' times.'

These sharp words worked to their purpose and caused me to collect myself. I cocked the pistol and then looked once more over the rock. As I did so, those with rifles and muskets began to open up on the oncoming riders. I knew that there was little to be gained from firing until the men were practically on top of us. Firing a pistol at a moving target at that distance would have been a waste of powder and lead. All I could do was wait until the enemy were closer.

Not so the woman next to me, who was firing and reloading every twenty seconds or so. So proficient was she with her musket that I was ashamed to recollect how long it had taken me to reload on the rare occasions when I had fired a rifle or scattergun. From the moment that we heard the first shot she maintained a steady rate of fire of perhaps three shots a minute, which I found astoundingly fast.

I looked one more time over the top

of the rock and was relieved to see that the riders were swerving away on both sides and that some had even turned tail to run. It was hard to be sure, but I didn't think that any of the shooting had been coming from them. If I didn't act fast, I would end up being the only one who had not discharged her weapon, and so I fired three times at the confused mass of riders who were now a hundred yards or so from us.

Then the one-sided battle was over and the remainder of their force had retreated, leaving twenty or thirty men and horses lying out on the plain. It felt like something of an anticlimax: hardly a fight at all. At the very least I had supposed that I might be able to shoot at close hand one of the warriors bearing down upon us. Instead, they had gone without a real fight.

I guess that I ought to explain what had happened, based on what was later known of the Comanche invasion that spring, otherwise readers will most likely be scratching their heads and asking why those boys just cut and run when the going got hot.

What had happened was this. Some medicine man had begun a crazy dance which, when undertaken, made the dancers invulnerable against the white men's bullets in battle. There were only two catches. First off was where those who had joined in this spook dance mustn't use any of the white man's ways themselves which, for starters, meant abjuring guns. This naturally put the Indians at a disadvantage when fighting in open battle.

The other thing was that the braves were only safe as long as they had perfect faith in the god or ghosts or whatever it was. If they wavered in their belief, then the bullets could slay them. When their friends were cut down in battle they could say to themselves: 'Oh, so and so didn't have as much faith as me. No wonder he's been killed!' Mind, I have seen this same line adopted by white Christians at river-crossing camp revival meetings, so it's not limited to the Indians!

After the Comanches had fled some of the men went out to tally up their losses. They counted twenty-seven dead men. Our side didn't lose a single person, sustained not even so much as a scratch. There was general cheerfulness and good-natured feeling all round after the Indians had left or been defeated or whatever you cared to call it.

Some of the men, and also one or two of the women, came over to make my acquaintance, word having spread that there was a young girl in britches who was a sight to see. Once again, young Rawlings was left in the shade and I could see him lurking in the background, looking sulky and discontented.

Now if I had been feeling better disposed towards Tom Rawlings, then I might have agreed either to stay in Eldorado a while longer or perhaps even to carry on down the trail with the soldier I somehow seemed to have hitched up with. As it was, I couldn't face the prospect of spending any more time in his company. He was cowardly, bad-tempered and as sulky as a bear. I was damned if I knew why I should not ditch him now that the opportunity had presented itself. After all, he was safe here and maybe some of the citizens of Eldorado would be able to lend him a hand.

For my own part, I had endured about as much of him as I felt able to do and since I owed him nothing, I resolved to start off south-east again, which was, as you will recall, my original plan before meeting up with Tom Rawlings.

That evening though, a couple of the town's folk insisted that we stay at least for the night. The woman I had been next to during the attack was called Martha Hammond and she would not hear of me going until she had had a chance to hear my tale. As was a regular feature now, she appeared to have considerably less time for Rawlings, asking bluntly, when he wasn't present,

'How come you pick up with a deserter?'

I ate with Martha and her family that evening, while Rawlings stayed in the company of Clinton, who appeared to be a bachelor. This suited me well enough, as I had had enough of Rawlings's company to last me a good long while. As we ate, Martha and her husband Chris plied me with questions and showed a flattering interest in all my adventures.

Martha had told him about my confessing to shooting dead the men who had set out to rob me. He asked me about this in some detail, listening quietly to my account, without evincing any sign of unfavourable judgement.

When he had heard the whole story, he nodded and said briefly, 'Good work!'

This made me swell with pride, which is a strange thing to say about what some would say amounted to a case of murder.

Martha and Chris gave me a

shakedown on the floor and I slept like a babe, not awakening until the sun had risen. My hosts would by no means hear of my leaving before they had furnished me with a good breakfast. As we ate, Martha asked what my plans were and when I told her I was leaving, she got to her feet and went off abruptly without saying why. I was anxious that I had somehow offended her, but she returned with a jute sack containing a loaf of bread, some cheese and one or two other things. I tried to decline, but her face grew so fierce that I came to the conclusion that it would be more polite to accept the gift graciously. I took affectionate leave of the Hammonds and then went over to collect my pony. There remained only the unattractive task of letting Tom Rawlings know that I would not be taking him with me on my travels.

'You can't just jettison me like a bit o' baggage you got no more use for!' exclaimed Rawlings, when once I had apprised him of my intentions, 'It ain't right.'

'Right don't enter into it,' I told him, 'I got business elsewhere and you'd only slow me down.'

'You think you're better than me, ain't that the truth of it? I see the way you been sucking up to everybody, makin' 'em all think you something special.'

'Never thought on it at all, you want the truth. It's nothing to me what folk think of you.'

When he could see that this tack wouldn't answer with me, he tried another tactic, saying, 'Ah come on, Beth. We get on fine. Don't leave me stranded here.' Since I had known him less than forty-eight hours in total, I hardly knew how to respond to this, so I didn't try.

Clinton had stashed my tack in a shed. I took it out and set about preparing the pony for travel. I knew that Rawlings was a little vexed with me, but I didn't realize quite to what extent until I took the saddle and bridle out to the pony and began tacking up. The young soldier trailed out after me, and as I was fastening the saddle girth he unexpectedly lashed out at me with his foot; catching me painfully in my ribs. I was momentarily winded, but by no means incapacitated, and instantly whirled round, ready to get to grips with him. I didn't get the chance, though.

By the time I had stood up and was ready to grapple with the young man who had taken me by surprise in this way, I glimpsed a flash of movement in the corner of my eye and the man called Clinton came charging out of nowhere to crash into young Tom Rawlings and send him sprawling in the dirt.

Before Rawlings had a chance to get to his feet, Clinton said, 'You young scoundrel! Kick a girl, would you? Stand up and take a kick at me now, if it's a fight you're after. By God, I never saw such a thing!'

'It's all right, sir,' I said, 'I can take care of my own self.'

'I don't doubt it for a moment, child. But I'll be da . . . I mean to say as I'll be blowed if I watch anybody kick a girl like that and not show 'em where they're goin' wrong.'

By this time I had the pony all ready to go and Clinton said to me, 'You're really off, are you? Well, you got more courage than any person your age I ever knew or heard of. Good luck.' As an afterthought, he added, 'This fellow not going with you?'

I shook my head and said, 'Not hardly.' Then I mounted up.

Clinton said, 'God bless you, girl. You take good care o' yourself, you hear what I tell you?'

'Goodbye, sir, and thank you.'

Having completed all the goodbyes that I felt the occasion demanded I was away, trotting down the slope which led out onto the plain.

Now that I was free of the encumbrance of a companion on foot, I was free to fly along at my own speed. It felt good to be free of the town and the people in it. All I wanted now was to get back to a Pony Express station and hand over the *mochila* to somebody working for the company. It had become something of a point of honour now, that I was going to make sure that no harm befell those letters with which I had been entrusted. This might perhaps sound strange, but I had really begun to think of myself as being an employee of the company. While they were in my care, those letters would not be tampered with or harmed.

The land stretching south was open grassland. To my right, which is to say the east, were hills and, rising behind them, some rocky-looking little cliffs: higher than hills but not quite mountains. I figured that if I kept riding south and then, when the opportunity presented itself, veered somewhat right, then I would be on the right trail. Unless my calculations were greatly out this should then bring me across the trail that I had taken when heading towards Smoky Mountain.

When you're young all life is an adventure, and when you are as young as I was then, then those adventures are more like something from a story book than from real life. Despite my life having been cast into hazard on more than one occasion in the days since leaving St Joseph, I was having a whale of a time and was still greatly excited at the prospect of telling my family all about the time I had had.

I was making good progress throughout the morning, trotting mainly, but breaking into a canter from time to time. The idea that there could be any more adventures, let alone danger, in store for me simply did not cross my mind. As far as I was concerned I was all but home and dry.

It was while I was in this felicitous frame of mind that my attention wandered from the task in hand and I failed utterly to notice the greatly increasing number of prairie-dog burrows, which dotted the grassy plain across which I was travelling.

I had been thrown by a horse before in my life, sustaining a broken collar-bone on one occasion, when I was much younger, but things had been going so free and easy that morning that it never for a moment occurred to me that such a misfortune might be about to strike me that day.

This turned out to be a mercy, for when the pony came to a dramatic and total halt I went sailing over his head as limp as a rag doll, having had no prior warning of anything untoward. The fact that I flew through the air and landed like that, so floppy, was what saved me from injury. When you're anticipating a tumble there is a natural tendency to stick out a hand to break the fall. This all too often results in a broken wrist or even worse.

As it was, I landed heavily on my side, winded but unhurt. It was only when I clambered to my feet and went to see what had happened that I realized that I was in some not inconsiderable trouble. The pony was lying, struck all of a heap and making pitiful whinnying noises suggestive of great pain and distress.

You didn't need to be a veterinarian to see at once that something was seriously amiss with the beast, for his right foreleg was twisted forward at an impossible angle. I could see at a glance that the leg was badly broken.

Now, much as I felt sorry for the horse, I was all too keenly aware of my own peril: stranded in the middle of nowhere with a large party of angry Comanches on the warpath somewhere not too far away. There was nothing to be gained from lingering there on that barren plain, where I was plainly visible for miles in any direction.

I was sorry that I had let the pony come to grief and it was also a matter of some regret that I should be compelled to abandon the mail which had been entrusted to me. The idea, though, of burdening myself with the *mochila* and trying to carry that along with me on foot was not to be thought of.

It remained only for me to perform a last service for the suffering animal, which was making feeble attempts to rise and then shrieking in agony when it moved its leg. I took out my pistol and cocked it. Then I went over to the horse and stroked his head.

I had seen a pony being destroyed like this before, but on that occasion I little thought that I would be called upon one day to perform this melancholy office myself. It took some time to grit my teeth and put the barrel of the gun into the creature's ear. There was another long pause before I could bring myself to squeeze the trigger.

10

The shot sounded strangely flat, there being nothing at all for it to echo from. I never knew a loud bang to fade away so swiftly and completely before. I holstered my pistol and then set to, rummaging through the saddlebag and thinking about what I had best take with me. One thing was certain-sure and that was that I would have to travel pretty damned light.

While I was engaged in sorting out my gear for what promised to be a long and arduous walk I chanced to glance up and see a lone rider heading straight towards me. So level and flat was the plain that I could see for several miles in any direction and I guessed that this person must be about two miles away. As can be imagined, I was feeling very vulnerable and exposed.

I stopped what I was doing and

turned my attention to whoever it might be who was coming in my direction. It was a mercy that there only appeared to be one rider, rather than a whole host; but then again, this might be merely a scout. Naturally, and almost as a matter of course, given recent events, I was thinking in terms of Indians at this point.

Not until the lone horseman was less than a quarter mile from me did I recognize him, and I was engulfed in a sense of enormous and overwhelming relief. It was just that miserable young trooper from Fort Richmond, who had apparently taken it into his head to dog my footsteps. When he was near enough, I hailed him, crying, 'Hidy, there! You following me or what?'

Tom Rawlings reined in and shot me a look for which I did not altogether care. He said, 'What's happened to you, Miss High and Mighty? You never hear that pride goes before a fall?' He chuckled unpleasantly and I could see that he still held some kind of grudge about the very different ways that the two of us had been treated back in Eldorado.

'How'd you acquire that horse?' I asked curiously.

'Just took it is all,' came the reply. 'I'm tellin' you, I had to ride hard to catch you up!'

'Took it? You mean you stole it?'

Rawlings shrugged his shoulders nonchalantly, saying, 'That don't signify.' He gave me a silly smirk.

At these words a chill went through me and I knew at once that I had been quite mistaken in my estimation of the young soldier. I had taken him for an amiable, if petulant, fool. I was wrong. He was likely to be dangerous.

Of all the misdemenours and offences one could commit in those days, few were regarded with more fury than the stealing of horses. Taking a man's horse could leave him stranded in the wilderness and at risk of death. In many places, horse-thieves were lynched more or less as a matter of course. This was especially likely to be the case in a tiny, out-of-the-way town like Eldorado, where the residents relied upon their horses for contact with the outside world. The fact that Rawlings was either indifferent to or unaware of this, was worrying and gave me to suppose that he was perhaps slightly mad or more of a menace than he had looked at first sight.

'You crazy or what?' I enquired. 'You stole a horse and don't think nothing of it? Boy, I think there's something wrong with you.'

My words hit home, because Rawlings narrowed his eyes and said, in a queer, tight voice, 'Don't you call me crazy, you stuck-up, trashy piece of goods. You'll see how crazy I am in a minute.'

Then it all made sense to me. This young fellow really *was* crazy and that was the explanation for all the erratic and unpredictable conduct that he had displayed. It also explained why he was now looking so all-fired mean about being called 'crazy'.

I said lightly, 'I was only joshing. Don't take on so.' I turned away and continued to poke about in the dead pony's saddlebag, trying to decide what to take with me.

This seemed to enrage Rawlings further, for he said, 'Don't you turn your back on me, like I don't mean aught.'

'I'm busy, Tom,' I said in as pleasant an voice as I could muster. 'I got a long journey ahead of me and I needs must make preparation for it.'

Out of the corner of my eye I could see that Tom Rawlings was dismounting and I knew then that I was in serious trouble. Here was a fellow who could hazard his neck by stealing a horse and think nothing of it. And I was stuck out here in the middle of nowhere with this mad young man; someone who was, from all that I was able to collect, nursing a big grudge against me. It was a tricky position in which to find myself.

I stood up and turned to face Rawlings, thinking that he would stop a certain distance from me and then say some angry things. Instead, he marched right up until his face was only a foot or so from my own. I observed that he was becoming red in the face and that he was also breathing heavily. In my own brother these signs and symptoms frequently signalled that he was about to lose his temper and so it proved in Rawlings's case.

He fairly shouted in my face, 'I ain't crazy! You just say it, you damned snot-nose. Say as I ain't crazy.'

If I'd been fooling round with my brother I would at this stage have taken him literally at his word and said, 'I ain't crazy.' I somehow thought that Tom Rawlings would not appreciate me playing games of that sort and that I'd do better trying to placate him.

I said, 'All right, I was only kidding. You ain't crazy. There, you happy now?' It appeared that Rawlings was anything but happy though, for his hand snaked out and he slapped me fairly hard around the face.

The shock of the blow spurred me into action and I knew now that here was a young man, taller and perhaps stronger than me, who was intent upon hurting or humiliating me over some fancied slight. Whether it was me or if perhaps he had been stung by what he perceived the attitude of the folk at Eldorado to be towards him, here was a man who was determined to show that he was the boss.

Perhaps a softer approach on my part would, even now, have smoothed things over, but I had never in my life allowed anybody to take the liberty of striking me and I was damned if I was going to make an exception for Tom Rawlings. I flung myself at him like a wildcat.

So taken aback was he by my assault that at first Rawlings gave back, raising his hands to protect his face after I had raked one cheek with my nails. It didn't take him long to counter-attack though, and when he did it was with considerably more vigour than I was accustomed to when in a rough-and-tumble with my brother. Rawlings swung a fist at my head and although I succeeded in deflecting it, I was thrown momentarily off balance.

Then he was on me, grabbing and punching. This furious onslaught took me by surprise and before I knew what was happening I had been shoved roughly to the ground and the young man, whom I had so gravely misjudged, was on top of me, fumbling with my clothing.

Until that moment, incredible as it might seem, I had not really known what was going on. I'd seen Rawlings's behaviour as obnoxious and thought that he simply wanted to slap me about a little in order to teach me a lesson. Now I could see where all this was tending. He was hoping to teach me a lesson all right, while at the same time satisfying his baser instincts. His clear intention was to force himself upon me.

The knowledge of this hit me like a hammer blow.

If anybody, man, woman or boy believed that they could take liberties with my person, then I was the one to disabuse them of such a notion. While Rawlings was concentrating on trying to pull down my pants I drew the pistol at my hip, cocking it as I did so. I presented the barrel to his face and said, 'You don't desist now, I'm going to blow your brains out.'

The young man stopped, but then said, 'You wouldn't dare!' Whereupon, without further ado, I pulled the trigger. Now although Rawlings palpably flinched as he heard the harsh, metallic click, it was not followed at once by the roar of gunfire. I cocked my piece and fired again, with the same result.

'Why,' said the young man triumphantly, 'you ain't even knowed enough to load the thing. If that's not just like a girl!'

This was just the sort of ill-considered and foolish remark that my own brother was apt to make. What one will tolerate from a close blood relative and what, on the other hand, one will endure from a stranger, are clean different things. I might put up with a comment like that from Jack; I certainly was not about to let this Tom Rawlings get away with such sassing.

All else apart, I was still in imminent peril of losing that precious jewel that, at least according to some fancy writers, is more dear than life itself to a well-brought-up girl. For that reason I swung my pistol against the side of the boy's head with all the force I could put into the blow. The effect of having two pounds of steel slam into his head was not all that I could have hoped and so I repeated the process twice more. By the third blow I had knocked Tom Rawlings out cold.

At first I feared that I had killed him, but when I bent my head down cautiously I found that I could just about hear him breathing. Not that I would have been overly distressed had I discovered that he was dead. I was faced with a choice, which was really no choice at all.

First off was where I could follow my original plan and set off on foot. This would mean that when Rawlings came to he would hop on that horse he had taken and come galloping after me, even madder than he had been before. This was not an attractive proposition.

Next, I could go off on foot after untacking the horse and setting it free. This would mean that Rawlings would be tracking me on foot.

Finally, I could comandeer his mount and leave him here to make his own way unmounted.

It is my belief that I was no more dishonest than anybody else, but I couldn't see that leaving Tom Rawlings in possession of that stolen horse would be of any benefit to the owner. Similarly, if I turned it loose it would be a hundred to one against the rightful owner ever seeing it again.

If, however, I took the beast for my

own self and rode it south, then I might be able to hand it over to a sheriff at some point and he could return it somehow to Eldorado.

That this scheme would also accord well with my own plans was neither here nor there. In the end, after engaging in all sorts of sophistry and self-justification, I took off the saddle and replaced it with the one from the dead pony. I also slung the *mochila* over the saddle, intent once again upon making sure that the mail got through.

If the Indians found Tom Rawlings lying out there alone and unprotected, then they would most likely make an end of him. This did not so much as even tickle my conscience. He had come damned close to taking advantage of me against my wishes and that was almost as bad as horse-thieving for most folk. So it was that I saddled up and left without so much as a backward glance at my erstwhile companion.

Those who think that I had no conscience at all for taking a stolen horse in this way and then abandoning somebody leaving him helpless in the middle of nowhere, will mistake my feelings entirely. I knew that I was not behaving as I had been raised to do; but then the circumstances in which I found myself were uncommon and the usual rules and regulations that govern the way we act in polite society had broken down.

It was a case of every man, or girl, for his or her self. Not wanting to die out there, hundreds of miles from home, I found that I had no alternative than to act like that.

As I cantered along I fell to thinking about my pistol and why it had misfired. The explanation was a simple one. In the all the excitement of the encounter at Eldorado, when I had fired a few shots at the backs of the departing Comanches, I must have fired not one or two, but three shots. This would account for my only having one loaded chamber ready when I wished to destroy my pony. The worst of it was that I had no powder or shot to reload. I would just have to hope and pray that I would have no cause to need a gun again until I was safe back home.

As the day wore on and the morning gave way to afternoon and then evening, I was beginning to be hopeful that either that day or the next I would strike the trail that I had passed along on the way to Smoky Mountain. There was no lack of fresh water to be had in streams and such, and the food that Martha had given me back in Eldorado was sufficient to hold body and soul together, at least for the time being. It looked as though I was going to make it in one piece after all.

The range of hills and low, rocky mountains still ran along to my right, preventing me from veering east at all. There might have been some path through those hills, but after the mishap that had felled my pony I was in no way inclined to take any chances. The trackless land across which I was riding was dull and flat, but as long as I kept my eyes open for any hazards such as holes or rocks, I thought that I'd be all right.

As it became obvious that the line of hills ran on without a break, I began to press further in that direction, riding closer and closer to the hills, so that I shouldn't miss any little pass which might allow me to head east.

By late afternoon or early evening I was riding up the gentle slopes that led into the hills. This meant that I was able to watch for anything in the nature of a track that might take me to the east and also, because the land was a little higher on the slopes, that I could see far across the plain.

I reined in and scanned the horizon for any sign of life. I was hoping that maybe I would stumble across another little town like Eldorado. What I actually saw, away to the left, was a tiny cloud in the distance. As I watched, it resolved itself gradually into a large party of riders, who were moving across the dusty and parched grasslands in my direction.

At first I hoped that this might be the column of cavalry that had set out from Fort Richmond, but by straining my eyes, I could just make out flashes of white and red on the heads of some of the riders. Unless I was altogether mistaken, these were eagle-feather war bonnets and it wasn't hard to figure out that they were worn by Comanche warriors who were now bearing down in my direction. It was hard to calculate, but I would say that there could have been as many as a hundred horsemen in total.

The nearby hills were an uninviting sight for a rider, growing increasingly steep and rocky once the gentle slope I was on came to an end. I gazed around in vain for any opening between the hills and rockfaces, through which I might be able to lead my horse. There was nothing. It was impossible to say whether the men heading towards me had yet caught sight of the lone rider up by the hills, but they surely would if they carried on along their present path.

I could not work out what to do for the best. Unless the men were actually coming up to these hills, and there was no real reason why they should do so, then they would most likely swerve off long before they got to me. Perhaps they knew of some pass which led through to the other side of the hills.

If I began to move now, though, the movement might catch somebody's eye and I might precipitate the very crisis which I was hoping to avoid. Since I had no present hope of passing over to the other side of the hills I chose, by default really, to remain where I was and hope for the best.

Sometimes, avoiding a decision and just letting nature take its course is not the best way of proceeding. So it proved that afternoon, because as they crossed the grassy plain, kicking up grey dust as they came, the Indians, who I was sure, now that I could see them closer to, numbered at least a hundred, showed not the least sign of deviating from their chosen direction. Which is to say that they carried on, heading straight for me.

It was too late to think of fleeing now, and when they were a half-mile or so from me some of the braves gave warbling cries of triumph, like hunters who have sighted the quarry. It was a spine-tingling sound, because on the present occasion the quarry was me.

There was no doubt that the men had seen me, because they were close enough now for me to see which way they were facing and every one of them appeared to be looking at me. It was an unenviable situation in which to find myself. I toyed briefly with the notion of galloping off madly, but it would have been sheer suicide. There was little I could do, other than bide my time and wait to see what developed.

I had all but given myself up for lost, when a sharp, clear sound rent the air; remote, but not so far away as to be indistinct. It was the brassy voice of a bugle.

The Indians below me heard the bugle as well and their reaction was swift; like a flock of birds they all wheeled together to face the source of the sound. Now, instead of coming on straight at me they were facing to the right, and when I looked that way as well I nearly fainted with joy.

There, about a mile further on from where I had so far reached, must be the pass for which I had been seeking. From the hills there rode a column of blue-coated cavalry, their sabres drawn and shining in the evening sun. They were the most splendid sight I had ever seen in my life.

So it was that I had what you might term a grandstand seat at one of the most famous actions of the Indian Wars, which was known in later years as the Battle of Hebden Pass. It was named after the pass through the hills and mountains that I had been looking for as I rode south that day.

The forces in the fight that I witnessed that day were more or less equal, with about a hundred men on each side. In fact there were slightly more soldiers than there were Indians, but only by a dozen or so.

Although it was called a battle by historians who wrote of this incident in later years, I can say honestly that it was more like a massacre. If the fighting had been between the troopers with their curved swords on side and the Indians with their lances and knives on the other, then the outcome might have been uncertain. The cavalry might have had an edge, due to their discipline, but then the Indians were utterly fearless and unafraid of death. As it was, there was no real fighting at all to speak of.

The horse soldiers rode on at a trot and then, at a signal from the bugler, halted. There was a shout of command from an officer at which, as one, they sheathed their sabres. I thought that this was a crazy move, for the Comanches were now heading towards them at a fair pace.

There was another command, which drifted to me on the evening breeze; it was too distant for me to make out the words clearly. The import of the order was plain though, for as I watched, every soldier reached back and withdrew from the scabbards on their saddles the short carbines hanging there.

There was only fifty yards now between the stationary line of cavalry and the charging Comanches. I heard one more barked command, then every one of those men on horseback raised his weapon and fired. Even at the distance away that I was the volley of shots sounded like a protracted roll of thunder.

The consequences of this were immediate and dreadful. Around three-fourths of the Indians and their horses were felled, tumbling heads over heels into the path of the other riders. Even those who had not been killed in that first round of firing found themselves thrown from their mounts as their horses' legs became entangled in the men and horses who had fallen from the gunfire.

Only a pitiful remnant of the charging braves reached the cavalry and were able to engage in hand-to-hand combat with the troopers. Even then, it was hardly a fair fight. Some of the soldiers drew their swords and fought in that way, but most simply used their pistols to deadly effect.

Within little more than a minute it was all over and every one of those hundred Comanches lay dead.

11

Horrified as I was at the unequal battle that I had witnessed, I could not help but be pleased and relieved that I was no longer menaced by such a large body of angry and bloodthirsty Indians. I was sorry, though, to see so many men killed like that in front of my eyes.

I spurred on my horse, riding swiftly down the slope to where the soldiers were now exulting in their victory. It was at that moment that I came more close to losing my own life than at any time since setting off from St Joseph. There was a cry of warning, followed almost instantly by the crack of a rifle being discharged. A bullet whistled past my head so close that I felt the wind of its passing.

What had happened, of course, was that one of the soldiers had seen a rider bearing down on him and his comrades and had assumed as a matter of course that it must be another Indian warrior. There were shouts of protest, though, at his rash action, as others saw that I was white. They suffered me to approach without firing at me again.

To my amazement I found that this was the column from Fort Richmond, under the command of Colonel Parker. At his side was his adjutant, Major Conway, and both men looked a good deal more travel-stained, dusty and weary than when last I had met them, only a few days earlier. For their part, they both appeared to be pleased to see me.

'Miss Taylor,' said Major Conway, 'I rejoice to see you in good health. I was a-feared that you had been killed in the attack on the fort.'

'No,' I replied pertly, 'it would take more than that to settle with me.'

The major smiled at that and said, 'Yes, I dare say that's true.'

Colonel Parker introduced a more formal tone to the conversation, by saying, 'I too am glad to see you, Miss Taylor. We owe you a debt of gratitude. However, I think that a young girl such as yourself has been wandering about unprotected for just about long enough. You'll travel south with us now, so that I might deliver you to the safekeeping of some responsible authority.'

If somebody had talked in this way of handing me over to any authority a day or two earlier I would have bridled and then fought tooth and nail against the idea. Now, though, it sounded quite reassuring and although I didn't say yea or nay to the scheme, I hoped that my silence would be taken for consent.

It was, and when the field of battle had been tidied up and provision made for the dead and wounded troopers, we all set off together through that pass which I had been seeking before the fighting had erupted.

The famous Battle of Hebden Pass, which features so much in histories of the State of Kansas, ended in the death of a hundred and twelve Indians. By stark contrast, only two soldiers were killed and nine injured. It was the first and only battle I have ever witnessed with my own eyes and I can truthfully say that it was a bloody and brutal business, which involved little heroism on either side.

Having recovered me, Colonel Parker seemed anxious that I should not go astray once more. I do not know if this was because of genuinely altruistic concern for my welfare as a young and vulnerable girl, or because he was worried that it would look bad for him if I ended up getting scalped by the Indians.

Whatever his motive, he detailed a trooper to ride alongside me and make sure that I did not get lost again. This man, a grizzled sergeant, was an amiable travelling companion and he appeared to be quite taken with me and my story.

'No, but did you really ride for that new Pony Express outfit?' asked Sergeant McDermott. 'But you're a rare one! How old d'you say you was?'

'Fifteen.'

'Lord, you're somethin' else again. Anyways, I got to make sure you don't go a-missin', so I hope you won't mind if I stick to you like a cockleburr?'

'You go right ahead,' I told him, and I meant it. It gave me a nice warm feeling to know that somebody was taking care of me until I could be returned to my mother. I had surely had enough adventures over those days to last me a lifetime.

Getting me home proved somewhat harder to do than the Colonel anticipated. My own take on the matter was that with a horse between my legs and a fresh charge of powder in all the chambers of my father's pistol, I could probably make it to St Joseph just fine. Indeed, I thought that I would be able to ride back eastwards for the Pony Express and that nobody would be any the wiser about the deception in which my brother and I had engaged.

It appeared, though, that there was

not the slightest chance of doing this. By now the Pony Express knew about the destruction of the station at Smoky Mountain and they had assumed that one Jack Taylor Esq. had been killed by the Indians. When the cavalry arrived with me at one of the little staging posts, one which I had passed through on the way to Smoky Mountain, there was general consternation. That I had, throughout all my vicissitudes and tribulations, managed to preserve the *mochila* with which I had started out from St Joseph was viewed as little short of miraculous.

The three men at the station could not decide what they were most amazed about: that I had succeeded in keeping the *mochila* intact and in my care or the fact that it was now generally known that I was a girl.

One said, 'You guarded the mail with your life. I reckon you're the best boy we ever had so far!' He grinned as he said this, so that I would not be offended at being called a boy.

Another of the men said, 'You riding back eastwards for us, I reckon?'

The adjutant from Fort Richmond, Major Conway, chipped in at this point and said, 'This child is riding nowhere for anybody. We're aiming to send her home as soon as may be.'

'Don't rightly know how that'll work,' said one of the Pony Express men doubtfully, 'There ain't no railroad or stage running from here to St Joseph. Only us. It's over a hundred and fifty miles as the crow flies.'

'Be that as it may,' said the major, 'this girl has done with riding for you. All else fails, she can ride along of us for a day or two, I guess.'

It turned out that the bulk of the men from Fort Richmond were bound for some other fort, whose name I cannot quite recollect. A certain number though — eighteen — were heading for the Missouri River. Major Conway was not among their number, for which I was sorry, but the party was headed by Sergeant McDermott, with whom I had got on well.

After camping out near to the Pony Express station the soldiers split up the next morning and I rode along with the men heading east.

Sergeant McDermott was a regular Tartar when it came to keeping his men in order. Before we set off that day he addressed the troopers thus: 'Some of you fellows might note as we have a young lady riding with us, which I'll allow is no a common thing. That being so, I tell you all that if I hear any dirt, cussing or talk of any kind which ain't fitting for a well-brought-up young lady to hear, then you'll answer for it. Is that clear?'

It was, seemingly, clear, because during those two days that I rode with the cavalry I did not have the least apprehension about any one of those men. They were curious about me, to be sure, but very polite and respectful. Not one of them took any liberties or even spoke roughly. That was, I think, a tribute to what a ferocious sergeant they had.

When we were near the Missouri we came to a small town, perhaps twenty miles from the river itself. I had passed through this place on my ride to Seneca. Sergeant McDermott sought out the sheriff there and outlined the case to him, impressing upon the man most forcefully that I had to be tended to like I was a piece of delicate china and got back safe to my folks in St Joseph. The sheriff, with something of an ill grace, accepted the commission, which also says something about Sergeant McDermott's way of running down all opposition and having his own way. The long and the short of it was that the sheriff agreed to take me to St Joseph himself and hand me over to my mother.

Incredible to relate, I arrived back at the ferry across the Missouri only a week after I had left for Seneca. It felt like a lifetime and I knew that, in some way, I had grown up over those days.

The man piloting the ferry stared at

me and my escort with a look that spoke of inquisitiveness, but seeing the sheriff with me caused him to hold his tongue. I don't rightly know what he thought was going on. I knew this man slightly, at least by sight, and wondered if he'd heard some tidings of what had been going on over in Kansas.

The sheriff said, when we had gained the far bank, 'I guess I'd better take you to the door, young lady. I don't want that firebrand sergeant on my tail, should anything miscarry with you getting home safe.'

We were both riding and I still hadn't told anybody the story of the horse I was on. I felt bad about the idea of hanging onto the beast and so I asked casually, 'You ever hear of a town called Eldorado?'

'Eldorado?' he replied, 'Sure. Boom town, or used to be. Silver. Why d'you ask?'

'No special reason. Only this horse belongs to somebody there.' He gave me a quizzical look and I added hastily,

226

'I didn't steal it. But happen you could return it there. I wouldn't feel good about keeping it.'

The sheriff looked as though he wished that I had not burdened him in this way and that he would have been happy not to be told about the horse, but he agreed to take it back across the river with him.

By this time, we had reached my home. I tried to dismiss the man with profuse thanks, but he was having none of this, it being his fixed intention of speaking a few words to mother and ensuring that I was now transferred into the care and protection of some responsible grown-up person.

There was nobody outside our house and so I dismounted, nervous, now it had come to the point, of what my mother's reaction would be to all this.

I soon found out. Just as I got down from the horse, the door to my home opened and out walked my ma. I had never seen her in such a state; her hair was down and her face chalk white.

She looked altogether distracted. Her clothes were in disarray and she was bent over like an old woman.

She did not at first look up to see me, so I cried out cheerfully, 'Hey, Ma! I'm back!' Whereupon my mother looked up quickly, her eyes widened to an astonishing degree and then she swooned clean away, crumpling up in a heap.

The sheriff hastened over to where my mother lay on the path and began trying to rouse her. I went over as well and then I heard my brother say, from behind me, 'Hidy, sis.' I turned round and there stood Jack.

He said, 'They said as you was dead. Killed by the Comanches, but I didn't believe a word of it. I knew for certain-sure you'd be back again.'

I noticed that Jack was standing on his two feet without any apparent difficulty, so I said, 'Your ankle better now?'

For a moment, my brother looked perplexed, like he didn't know what I was talking about. Then he said, 'Oh, that. No, it's fine now. Sprain weren't as bad as I feared.'

'Oh, that's a mercy,' I said. 'Happen you'll be in a position to take over from me now at the Pony Express?'

'I wouldn't o' thought so,' he said gloomily, 'Everybody knows about that stunt we worked.'

'Oh? How's that?'

At this point my mother recovered consciousness. Despite the sheriff telling her not to stir but to stay lying down, she got unsteadily to her feet and enfolded me in the tightest embrace I have ever received in my life, clinging on to me desperately as though she was a drowning sailor and I a rock.

She said, 'I been plumb distracted, child. I thought you was dead.'

At some time during this affectionate family reunion the sheriff slipped away, taking with him, as well as his own mount, the horse I had acquired from Tom Rawlings. My mother led me, still hanging onto me, as though unwilling to let me leave her side.

What had happened was that the Pony Express riders travelling east had swiftly brought tidings of the attack at Smoky Mountain and the fact that a bunch of dead bodies were found there. Each new rider who fetched up in St Joseph added something to the tale and since all that was known was that I had ridden west from Seneca and had not been seen since leaving the way station fifteen miles east of Smoky Mountain, the conclusion was inescapable.

There isn't much more to say about this mad escapade of mine. We all, that is to say me and my mother and brother, thought that the Pony Express company would be furious at the deception practised on them, but in fact the publicity they received from all this was a prime factor in their success that year. The story of how one of their riders went racing off to alert the army to the Comanche invasion caught the imagination of the public and stories about it appeared in newspapers as far away as Washington and New York. That it had been a young girl, masquerading as a boy, served only to make the whole thing more curious and remarkable. The *mochila* that I had kept safe also featured in these tales.

Best off was where William Russell was so tickled by the business that he allowed my brother Jack to take up his job after all, now that his ankle was better. One of his riders being instrumental in the events which climaxed with the Battle of Hebden Pass was something to savour and Russell wished to present himself publicly as a man who appreciated grit of that sort.

That incident in 1860 was the only truly remarkable thing ever to occur in my life. Two years later I met and swiftly fell in love with the man I was to marry and my life since then has been blessed with normality and dullness.

Every so often though, somebody will remark of me to a stranger, 'That's Beth Taylor, as was. The only girl who ever rode for the Pony Express.'

We do hope that you have enjoyed reading this large print book.

Did you know that all of our titles are available for purchase?

We publish a wide range of high quality large print books including:
Romances, Mysteries, Classics
General Fiction
Non Fiction and Westerns

Special interest titles available in large print are:
The Little Oxford Dictionary
Music Book, Song Book
Hymn Book, Service Book

Also available from us courtesy of Oxford University Press:
Young Readers' Dictionary
(large print edition)
Young Readers' Thesaurus
(large print edition)

For further information or a free brochure, please contact us at:
Ulverscroft Large Print Books Ltd.,
The Green, Bradgate Road, Anstey,
Leicester, LE7 7FU, England.
Tel: (00 44) **0116 236 4325**
Fax: (00 44) **0116 234 0205**

NOLAN'S LAW

Lee Lejeune

After his mother and father die, and the girl he hopes to marry turns him down, Jude James decides to abandon his rented homestead and ride for the West along with Josh, a young exslave seeking sanctuary. Eventually they fall in with a gang led by Brod Nolan, who claims to rob the rich to feed the poor. But there is more to this than meets the eye — and the two friends find themselves embroiled in a series of bloodcurdling encounters in which they must kill or be killed . . .

PIRATES OF THE DESERT

C. J. Sommers

The locals call the sand dunes of the Arizona Territory southland a white ocean. One man, Barney Shivers, carries the comparison a little further when he orders his men to attack any freight shipping that he does not control, and steal the goods on board. A little old lady, Lolly Amos, contracts her nephew, Captain Parthenon Downs of the Arizona rangers, to fight back. Downs eagerly takes on the challenge — but little does he realize that his decision will draw him into a war against two bands of pirates . . .